# Candy Apples

Aleksander E. Petit

Copyright © 2026 by Aleksander Petit

*All rights reserved. No part of this book may be reproduced in any manner whatsoever without written permission except in the case of brief quotations embodied in critical articles and reviews.*

First Printing, 2026

ISBN (paperback): 979-8-9851804-3-5
ISBN (ebook): 979-8-9851804-2-8

Typography: Times New Roman, Lobster 1.4

*Life is like an apple;*
*if you don't enjoy it to its fullest,*
*it will rot in your hands.*

# *Prologue*

Miłosz Jagoda imagines that every high school is a bit like this: stifling, encasing, a papier mache shell to break your way out of.

For his residency, Miłosz worked at a small school in a small town. His own graduating class had been the size of this school's entire student body. It was supposed to be a quiet start to his teaching career.

When he wasn't offered a permanent position at the end of his time there, he wasn't surprised, but he wasn't disappointed either.

The plan after that was to start over somewhere new. New town, new school, a place big enough to understand that different doesn't need to be a bad thing.

He finds his way home instead.

Miłosz hadn't planned to move back to his hometown.

At first, it was just a brief visit at the start of summer as a break from job-searching. Most schools he applied to for an art teacher's position were "concerned" about his "effect on impressionable young minds," as if being transgender was a disease. He hadn't even been looking for a job during what was supposed to be a short stay.

Then his dziadzio got sick, and leaving became a non-option.

Which led Miłosz here, to a place he thought he'd never return to, getting paid to be here five days a week.

It's strange to work alongside the same people who taught him nearly a decade ago. The fact that they knew Miłosz pre-transition is disconcerting. At 5'6 with long curly hair, he doesn't look much different now than he did then.

"My first week was fine," Miłosz insists, sitting at his dziadzio's bedside. The air in the room is stale despite the open window, and there's a sharp clinical smell that no amount of air freshener can hide.

Dziadzio doesn't say anything back, of course. He hasn't been able to for a while. But he smiles the same smile as always, and that's enough.

# Chapter One

It's hard to choose a favorite color as an art teacher. There's beauty in every one of them, if you look at them the right way. Miłosz can't pick a single color that sticks out to him, even when put on the spot. No candy apple red or autumnal orange stands out like a beacon.

That being said, he's always been partial to greens.

His childhood, the part of it before they came to the United States, was spent on the sprawling, lush green of his dziadzio's farm. There were dozens, maybe hundreds, of shades of green to bask in. Grass, trees, freshly grown produce and their blooms.

Miłosz's mother passed sage green eyes down to him. He tries not to think about where they came from.

Green is the color on his brush now, the deep emerald of thick foliage. Their current unit in this class, a simple introductory drawing course, is on perspective. He practices that now on the piece he plans for them to study at the end of the unit.

Today's painting is nostalgic. His memories of home are hazy with age, but a collection of photographs reminds him of the finer details. Green on green on green.

A student asks a question. Miłosz drops his brush, wipes paint-splattered hands on a paint-splattered apron, and drags his focus back to the classroom.

The student is struggling with how to apply perspective.

Sometimes Miłosz feels the same way.

Miłosz has built a routine in the month or so that he's been working here. Routine steadies him, helps him feel grounded when the world rushes around him like crashing waves. As a teacher, he needs to be adaptable, but even that can be planned around to an extent.

This is not something he could have planned for.

"If it's too much trouble, though, don't worry about it!" The other teacher brushes their bangs back, a nervous gesture if not for the calm cool of everything else about them. "I'm sure I could scrounge something else up if necessary. This just seems like the best place to start."

Zhéng Tāo is the most talked-about teacher on staff. They're known for being friendly, handsome, and helpful, but only in a negative light. They're *too* friendly, handsome, and helpful, so the other teachers often smile to their face and then throw barbs behind their back. It itches to hear.

# CANDY APPLES

This is only the third time Miłosz has met Mx. Zhéng, but he has a few guesses as to why people give them trouble, and it's a reason Miłosz knows well.

The first time the two met was during new teacher orientation. Miłosz was one of two new hires this year, and Mx. Zhéng had volunteered to help with onboarding. They offered a tour, Miłosz declined since he already knew the school's layout, and that was that.

Their second meeting was in the teachers' lounge a few weeks later. Two teachers who have been around since long before his student days were spreading the rumors that seem to follow Mx. Zhéng around. Miłosz grabbed his food from the communal refrigerator and made a parting comment that they should hold their tongues for anything short of kindness. Obviously, if he chose confrontation, even as a parting blow, it had been a bad day for him. Mx. Zhéng was standing outside the door. They offered a fragile smile, Miłosz gave a swift nod, and the two went their separate ways.

This time, the theater teacher wants a favor.

"Check the storeroom," Miłosz offers with a wave of his hand. The empty one, to avoid paint splatter. "Pick out whatever you need, but please let me know what you take before you leave."

Mx. Zhéng gives a bright thanks that Miłosz doesn't turn away from his canvas to see.

The piece is nearly done despite having fought him every step of the way. Dense foliage frames the silhouette of his childhood home, lending it an eerie rather than homely feel. Foreboding instead of friendly. At this point, he just needs it *done*.

"What were you going for?"

The voice over his shoulder is a shock, jolting the hand holding his brush. A splash of viridian cuts through the image on the canvas.

Miłosz spills a few choice words that he would never use in front of his students, even the ones who don't know Polish, and wonders how he could possibly salvage this.

"I am *so* sorry! Is there any way to fix it?"

No, but looking at the marred mockery of the place he loves most, Miłosz isn't sure that anything could have fixed it even before. This is a perfect excuse for the restart he's been stubbornly denying.

"I was determined to make it work," he admits, more to himself than the person fretting over his shoulder, "but I don't think anything could have saved it."

A pause, then, "Is that a no?"

Their tone is so confused that Miłosz has to laugh. Not *at* them, never *at* someone, but laughing all the same. It's a small, unfamiliar thing that makes his throat tingle. He hasn't had a reason to laugh in a long while.

"No, there's no way to fix it other than starting over." A new start, the same thing he's been both striving for and struggling with. The only way to achieve it is through the same lesson he's been teaching his students: a shift in perspective.

Miłosz finally turns to his coworker, if only to catalog their spoils.

Mx. Tāo stands tall like a pillar of perfection in the center of art room chaos. Their dark hair is short and combed, swept in waves across their forehead. Crisp powder blue shirt, straight grey slacks, squared shoulders. Tidy.

Miłosz has never been so put-together in his life.

The other teacher's expression is strange, though. At odds with the rest of them. Rosy cheeks, wide eyes, slack mouth. Shocked, maybe, though Miłosz can't begin to guess why.

"What did you take for your project?"

That snaps them out of their haze. Mx. Zhéng smiles the same plastic smile they wear around the halls. "I hope this isn't too much." Everything goes onto the nearest table to inventory.

Miłosz catalogs it all on a sticky note using small, uniform cursive. The materials picked out are minimal: several sheets of construction paper, a set of colored pencils to be returned at a later date, and a few bits and bobbles that Miłosz hadn't known were in the storeroom in the first place.

"The previous art teacher would help with my projects," the theater teacher explains when asked. "Mr. Erikson would help me with set design and props when he had the time and gave me materials or feedback when he didn't. Of course, you're not obligated to do any of that; it's just the kind of person he was."

An encouraging smile and hands smeared with oil pastels. Lunch hours spent in companionable silence. Kind words in a letter of recommendation for college. An uplifting note waiting on the desk for Miłosz's first day on the job, tiny rainbow flag set beside it. *Art is a forgiving subject,* it said. *Are you?*

"I know."

Confusion takes over Mx. Zhéng's face. "You know?"

As a newer teacher, it's not surprising that they don't know about the years Miłosz spent here in his youth. When he turned down the tour for new teachers, he never stated why. The number of teachers who've started here in the eight years since he left can be counted on one hand. The rest know far more about his past than he's comfortable with.

"I was a student here." Softer, he adds, "It was a lifetime ago." He shakes the thought away; no point lingering on the past. "Anyway, take what you need, just don't forget to return what you can."

Mx. Zhéng leans against the desk, the picture of nonchalance. "When can I do that? Are you usually here late?"

No. There are guests over, and Miłosz has never been fond of guests. "I usually arrive an hour before school starts and leave an hour after it ends. You can return things during these times, or I also have third period free."

It's nearing 6pm now, much later than the 3:30pm he typically leaves by. The sun has started to dip but hasn't descended fully yet. Light casts the beige walls of the art room in purples, pinks, and blues. It spills across Mx. Zhéng, too, making their warm smile glow.

"What if I want to stop by but don't have anything to return? Can I still stop by then?"

## CANDY APPLES

It takes a moment for Miłosz to recognize the friendly overture for what it is. The last time someone tried to befriend him, Miłosz had been an undergrad. He isn't looking for friends any more now than he had been then.

Miłosz turns away to avoid seeing their reaction. He busies his hands with the flag on his desk, smearing it with green. "No." To hopefully soften the blow, he adds, "I prefer to focus on my work."

"Of course," they reply, voice soft. Disappointed but understanding, like rejection is a familiar blow they have learned to take. "Thank you for the supplies and your time. I'll return things as soon as I can."

With that, the theater teacher leaves without an ounce of drama.

The art teacher tries to go back to his work, but there's nothing to be done. The painting was a lost cause from the start.

He abandons the project for now. It can wait until another day—one when he can view it from a new perspective with a clear mind.

Right now, all Miłosz can think of is the soft awe on Mx. Zhéng's face the first time he really looked at them and the plastic smile slipping off as they turned away to leave. Something about it leaves him feeling wrong-footed with no idea as to why.

Miłosz never intended to plant roots here. He refuses to let this change his mind.

# Chapter Two

Miłosz likes his job, most of the time.

This is not one of those times.

He became a teacher to help kids, offer them a safe space in the middle of adolescent chaos. Being an art teacher lets him accomplish that while doing something he loves every day. It's a great position to be in. Most of the time.

Mr. Miłosz Jagoda is not immune to the horrors of teacher-guardian conferences.

"There is no reason for my child to be failing something as ridiculous as an art class!" This woman has been yelling for five minutes straight. Another five and Miłosz won't have time to breathe before his next appointment.

Teacher-guardian conferences are the speed-dating of torture. Each meeting is a slightly different trial of his patience than the last. Thankfully, this early bonus round is only for seniors to help keep them on track for graduation.

As a student, Miłosz's were always the same. His mother would spend every second trying to figure out why her child wasn't the perfect student and blaming everyone from the principal to the custodians.

A healthy mix of As and Bs wasn't good enough for her. Nothing ever was.

He sees an echo of her now in this screaming face.

"As I've said, the only way to fail this course is by not completing the coursework." This is his third time explaining this to her, the eighth time he's said it tonight.

"And as I've said, you are wrong! My son would never just not do his work!"

Green eyes flick to the student beside her. He hasn't finished a single assignment since the semester started, and he obviously couldn't care less.

Miłosz stands, signaling the end of the meeting despite a handful of minutes left. "The syllabus handed out at the start of the year was clear; the only way to fail is by not participating. Your son, like every student, has the opportunity to hand in late work for partial credit. Now, I must move on to my next meeting. Have a nice day."

The obvious dismissal is enough to send the woman into a sputtering rage. No words come out, though, and she and her son finally leave.

Which gives Miłosz a short reprieve before facing the same song and dance all over again.

He takes advantage of the impromptu break to stop by the teachers' lounge. Coffee has never been a vice of his, but it's stocked with tea and an electric kettle as well.

Approaching the room, he can hear the kettle already whirring. Hopefully with enough for two since he's on a time constraint.

The lounge is mostly empty. Meetings are scheduled through the evening, and their proper break isn't for another hour. The only other person here, prepping a mug on the counter, is as recognizable for their blue cardigan as their tidy dark hair. They don't turn as Miłosz comes in. They don't acknowledge him at all, though it's understandable given how they get along with the rest of the staff. Miłosz wouldn't have stopped what he was doing to greet someone either.

"Hello," Miłosz offers. He doesn't usually interact with the other staff when in here, but it's the only way he might get tea before he's due back. "Is there enough for two?"

Mx. Zhéng turns, a smile on their face but their eyes so tired. "Hey, yeah, of course. It's almost done."

The silence as Miłosz prepares his own mug is stifling. Silence is usually a familiar friend, but he can't shake the feeling that he did something wrong the last time they spoke. It's only been a few days. He's been stewing in it without understanding why.

"How is your project going?" The olive branch comes out softer than intended. It's barely above a whisper and, with the beep and whir of the kettle switching to warming mode, it might not be loud enough to hear.

They do hear it, though, and their smile widens just a fraction. Unnoticeable unless you were already looking. "It's going well. Some students are helping for extra credit and doing a great job. You're welcome to stop by the auditorium and see the posters sometime if you'd like."

Miłosz turns to his mug. It's peppermint with honey, the only thing they stock that he'll drink. He pours water over the teabag and watches how it starts to float up but doesn't fully make it. He feels like that sometimes. Often. Now.

The obvious answer is no. The *correct* answer is no. So why isn't that what comes out of his mouth?

"Maybe." Followed by the excuse of, "I don't spend much time outside of the art department." Seeing how his classroom *is* most of the art department, the excuse holds as much water as his maybe.

It's not a no, though. Miłosz curses himself for that.

Mx. Zhéng prepares their own drink. Miłosz wonders if they're using it as the same excuse to look away that he did. "I would offer to bring them by your classroom, but I wouldn't want to interrupt your work. Anyway, enjoy the tea and good luck with your meetings."

They leave without a parting glance. No plastered-on smile, no flash of tired eyes. Nothing.

For the first time, Miłosz wonders if his plan is stupid. This person obviously wants to be his friend, and here he is shooting them down in the most cowardly way possible. It feels idiotic. *He* feels idiotic.

But not enough to change his mind.

The tea tastes bitter on his tongue. Miłosz drinks it anyway.

# ALEKSANDER E. PETIT

The meetings continue.

Miłosz buoys himself with the knowledge that their dinner break approaches. When it arrives, he'll grab his food from the lounge and bring it back to his classroom. With everyone taking their break at the same time, the small handful of tables in there are sure to be crowded. Even at times they're not, he refuses to stay. Not that anyone has bothered asking him to, which is for the best.

His final meeting before the break runs late, a father proud of his son and hoping to help his child find opportunities. There was so much positivity and pride in him that Miłosz didn't even attempt to cut the man off. Miłosz did everything he could for them and ended the meeting feeling lighter than he had all night.

That feeling doesn't last. As expected, the teachers' lounge is crowded. A majority of the school's staff is crammed into the small space. Why more of them didn't retreat to their classrooms like he plans to is a mystery.

There are five tables. They're meant to have five chairs each, but one is crammed with six, another seven. In the corner is the table that people usually flock to because it's tucked away from prying ears. Most of the chairs are missing.

One of the remaining chairs is empty. The other seats Mx. Zhéng. The message is clear.

Everybody else is well into their food, so Miłosz has no trouble accessing the microwave to heat up his own. It's close to the noisiest of tables, so once it's started, he retreats to the only quiet corner of the room.

"Rough meeting?" Mx. Zhéng asks, long fingers stained orange by the fruit they're peeling. Miłosz shifts his gaze to the rest of their lunch: an empty container, half-empty plastic bags of baby carrots and veggie chips, and a reusable water bottle plastered with stickers.

The non-bee-nary one with a bee in the nonbinary pride flag colors is Miłosz's favorite.

"No," Miłosz admits, leaning against the empty chair but refusing to sit. He hadn't meant to open himself up to a conversation, but work talk couldn't hurt. Right? "It was good, actually. Otherwise, I wouldn't have let it run so long. I've never seen a parent so genuinely proud of their child."

Dziadzio has always been proud of him, and Miłosz will be forever grateful for that support, but he will also forever wish that dziadzio hadn't been the only one.

"I don't see many of those either." Mx. Zhéng drops the orange onto a napkin. They use empty hands to talk. "As a theater teacher, I mostly get guardians who think the subject is pointless or are very pushy about their kid becoming a star. There isn't much of an in-between."

The microwave beeps, butting off their conversation.

Mx. Zhéng hands Miłosz a plastic smile with wavering eyes. "You're welcome to eat here, but I'm sure you'd prefer to return to your classroom." Their tone is calm, sincere, despite the right

Miłosz believes they have to be petty. Instead of letting Miłosz dig his own grave deeper, they're offering him an out.

Miłosz thinks about that table as he crosses the room. Chairs removed, a single empty seat left behind for company. The blatant avoidance of a person who has only ever been kind. Sitting alone, not entirely by choice.

For Miłosz, it has been a choice. He's made no attempt to befriend the other staff.

Mx. Zhéng has attempted three times now to befriend Miłosz, each time more tentative than the last. How many times have they been turned away to sit alone at that table? How can they be brave enough to keep trying?

Miłosz can't sit at that table. The room is loud enough to make his ears buzz and ring, and the world feels fizzy in a way that itches. He recognizes the signs of overstimulation and knows that staying here longer than necessary will flip a switch that he keeps firmly taped down at work. He *can't* sit at that table.

But neither can they.

He strides up to the table, standing behind the empty chair and gripping the back with a white-knuckled hand.

"I'm going to eat in the art room." The tentative hope on Mx. Zhéng's face slips away, eyes cooling to neutral glass. It forms a lump in Miłosz's stomach that he hopes his next words will ease. "Would you like to join me?"

The lost hope is replaced by something else, warm but brittle, and Miłosz can't bring himself to think of this decision as a mistake.

## CANDY APPLES

They pack up their things with orange-tinted fingers. "Yeah. Yeah, that'd be great."

The pair walks in silence. It makes the whispers following them seem even louder, and Miłosz fights not to flinch at the attention. One or two people he could shake off, but here he feels like an ant against an army.

Things are much more peaceful once they reach the hallway. It's odd to walk beside someone like this; he's not used to how companionable it is, and it makes him nervous. Miłosz has no idea what to do.

He never does, though, so it's not much different than any other time.

"How is your dinner?" Miłosz asks, struggling to think of anything else to say. Not that he has to say anything in the first place, but the silence is digging under the collar of his dress shirt with clawed fingers.

Mx. Zhéng chuckles, honey in warm tea. "It's nothing special, mostly snacks to tide me over. A full stomach would have me half-asleep for the rest of my meetings."

Miłosz takes a second to rethink the container of pasta in his hands. It's worth it, he decides. There's nothing else for him to eat anyway.

They make it to the art room and deposit their food on the nearest table. The room is tidier than usual for the guests, supplies tucked away and tables wiped down. Still, there's no way to fully sanitize the chaos of an art room; the floor is forever smeared with paint and glitter.

"You haven't changed it much." Mx. Zhéng takes it all in with calculating eyes. Miłosz feels uncomfortably seen, despite them being right; he hasn't done much to personalize the space since moving into it.

"I didn't feel the need to," he admits. All his spare time in high school was spent in this room as it is now, charming in its mess but not very personal. A space anyone could find comfort in if they tried. "I like how it's always been."

The other teacher points to the pride flag on his desk and the mug it resides in. "The only thing that's changed is the mug. Even the flag is the same."

"The flag was a gift, and the mug I bought at a thrift store." It's a garish thing, in all honesty, and he's not sure what possessed him to buy it. The body has thick rainbow stripes with a white handle and text. It reads 'DREAM GAY' in big, blocky letters. Not the most professional desk decoration, but it's the kind of clear support his queer students need.

"It didn't cause a fuss tonight?"

It did. Miłosz is openly transgender, though; he's no stranger to queerphobia. He has long since learned to hold his own against it.

"I have it handled."

Miłosz doesn't say much after that, having no words or energy to force it. Mx. Zhéng fills the air with random chatter that Miłosz would normally find grating. Like this, in his safe space with a comforting voice, he doesn't mind. It's soothing like music with the way their voice swells and lulls. Maybe they were right about the heavy meal making him tired.

The break goes better than expected, even with Miłosz half-asleep. Mx. Zhéng talks with their hands, Miłosz listens while lazily scooping pasta into his mouth, and nothing bad happens. The world doesn't fall apart because Miłosz deviated from his plans.

Miłosz hasn't had companionship like this for so long that he forgot to miss it. He's not sure how he's going to fare once this little bubble of peace is popped.

Time runs out, as it always does.

Mx. Zhéng glances at their watch, and the smile that has blossomed on their face over the past twenty minutes fades. "I should go. There can't be a teacher-guardian conference without the teacher."

The joke is weak, and so is Miłosz's returning smile. As foolish as it was to do this in the first place, he had a nice time. He wishes he could let it happen again.

But he won't, so he savors this.

"Thank you." It's a concession that hurts his chest to make. "Good luck with your meetings."

"You too."

The sweet smile they send his way haunts him through the rest of the evening, through returning home to recount the night to his dziadzio, through the weekend that follows.

Come Monday, teacher-guardian night is a thing of the past, and Miłosz vows not to slip up again. No matter how tempting it is.

# Chapter Three

Perspective is something that Miłosz has never struggled with as an artist. It makes sense to him in a way that math or geography never could. Even other aspects of art, like color theory, took effort. But perspective was always a natural talent of his.

In art.

In the rest of his life, he's struggled with it, especially in his youth. Being a questioning then closeted trans kid was a struggle, and the only available perspective at the time was the one that kept him safe. College allowed him more freedom, but on a set path. Graduation gave him a truer sense of freedom.

Except he still ended up back here.

Miłosz does not regret the decision. He will always put his dziadzio first, even if it means making a home out of the town that chewed him up and spit him out.

That's the part he struggled with the most these days: viewing this city as a home. It's a perspective he's never been able to see, the reason he left the first time.

The reason he's not sure that he'll stay, when all is said and done.

Leaving will be easier if he doesn't give himself any reasons to stay. He's worked so hard to build a wall around his heart with no doors, no windows, to let people in.

And all it took to crack that resolve was a theater teacher with bulldozer kindness.

Miłosz had promised himself that he wouldn't slip up again, wouldn't let Mx. Zhéng get any closer. The moment of weakness would be just that: a moment.

Yet he's ended up somewhere unexpected once again.

It was innocuous at first, Mx. Zhéng coming by the art room to return leftover materials. Just some markers, the first time, with the excuse that they still had work to do with the other supplies. They explained how the process was going, and the art teacher in Miłosz couldn't resist offering feedback. It was more work than conversation, and Miłosz let himself have it.

Two days later, Mx. Zhéng returned with something else as a weak excuse to get more advice, ask more questions. Miłosz let himself ignore that the questions were more personal in how they asked for opinions. Still mostly work-related, though, so Miłosz brushed it off.

There's no excuse for how he ended up outside of the auditorium with an armful of art supplies after the final bell.

It was bothering him, something Mx. Zhéng said during their last conversation about painted posters deteriorating. That wasn't the focus of the conversation—it was the colored pencil posters being finished—so he hadn't put too much thought into it at the time. But today, one of his classes moved on to watercolors for an exercise, and it brought the issue to mind.

The paper type didn't match the medium. An obvious error he should have caught on to sooner. The excuse he's made for himself to be here, because at this point things have gone too far to deny it, is that any further delay would result in unnecessary waste of materials. As a public school teacher aware of their meager budget, he can't allow that.

Which has led him to the open auditorium door, lingering uncertainly outside.

Technically, he had been invited once upon a time. There's no guarantee that the welcome has extended this long. Miłosz spends agonizing minutes standing, there debating whether or not to go in.

"You're a roadblock, Mr. J."

Miłosz stiffens, careful not to startle and drop his things. He turns to the familiar voice and is both relieved and mortified by one of his own students finding him like this.

Babelyn is bright-eyed and bushy-tailed as usual. With their sunny disposition and tendency towards sunflower motifs, they're a bright spot in his first-period Intro to Painting course. A slow learner but dedicated.

"Apologies." Miłosz steps aside, clutching the art supplies to his chest. "I'm looking for Mx. Zhéng."

The smile Babelyn sends him, though perfectly polite on the surface, screams danger. "I'm sure they'll love that. Follow me." They flap an oversized sleeve towards the door and walk away without checking that he follows.

He does, of course, like a duckling to the gallows.

"Z, I brought a guest!"

There's a sigh from the stage, projected larger than Miłosz has ever vocalized anything in his life. "You had better not be covered in grass stains and carrying a rabbit when I turn around."

The mental image that evokes is horrific in its comedy: Miłosz standing there with an oversized pocket watch proving him a tardy rabbit, an out-of-place figure in his Sunday best. A small, incongruous detail in the big picture.

Babelyn turns to him with a devious smile. "You would tell me if you were a rabbit, wouldn't you, Mr. J?"

Miłosz rolls his eyes to play along. "Of course not, Babelyn." His voice is wispy where theirs are solid. It barely carries at all. "It wouldn't be a very well-kept secret if I shared it. You will have to live with the mystery."

Little moments like this are his favorite thing about teaching. This child trusts him to be fair when joked with, when teased. It's a foundation he built with gentle hands and paint tubes for building blocks.

Is Babelyn a menace? Absolutely. And they're one of Miłosz's favorite students for it. He can't imagine being anywhere near this open at their age, despite his own mentor's encouragement.

Babelyn's laugh, bright and bubbling, clues Mx. Zhéng in on Miłosz's quiet response. The teacher turns, mouth poised open for a question, and freezes.

This is the most disheveled that Miłosz has seen them. Sleeves pushed up haphazardly and slipped halfway back down, clothes and skin smudged with dust, face flushed from exertion. Looking at the stage around them, Miłosz suspects that it's due to lugging boxes up from the trap door storage underneath.

Even looking a true mess, they're unfairly handsome. Miłosz is too awed to be jealous.

He's also endeared by the thick mystery smudge along their cheekbone, though he refuses to admit it.

Both teachers stare, waiting for the other to speak. Neither does.

"If you're done, can I get back to work?"

Done with what, Miłosz doesn't know, but the moment is broken.

Mx. Zhéng dusts off their slacks with dustier hands and straightens their back. "Of course. I've brought up most of the boxes, if you want to start with these."

"What, no thank you for the delivery?"

Their face keeps steady with a default smile. "Back to work, Babelyn."

The student walks past Miłosz with a wink and nudge that sets Miłosz's face on fire, but he studiously ignores them. Perhaps Babelyn will miraculously forget every moment of this embarrassing encounter if he never brings it up.

Hopefully, Mx. Zhéng can do the same.

In case neither of those things happen, though, Miłosz tries to salvage what little dignity he has left. He bundles it into his hands with the art supplies and stretches his arms out in offering.

It may not be the first time that Miłosz has put himself out there, that was in the teachers' lounge when he couldn't stand to see a single figure alone at that table, but this feels like the more important one. Despite his deflections and denials, he's still making a *choice*.

"I have a solution to your watercolor problem."

For some reason, Miłosz expects to be turned away. It's an irrational thought, he knows, given how steadfast the kindness of the other teacher has been. His hands tremble with nerves anyway.

Mx. Zhéng's face finally settles into something softer. First the shock, then the teacherly placidness. Miłosz hasn't seen a glimpse of the Mx. Zhéng he, admittedly, barely knows since stepping into their domain.

"That would be brilliant! Babelyn has been *so* frustrated that they can't figure it out." The teacher strides over to the edge of the stage, trailing a cloud of dust, and sits with legs dangling. "Thank you for coming by. I know you don't like leaving the art department, so it means a lot."

Blush rushes across Miłosz's cheeks. The occasions on which he receives thanks or praise are few and far between. It tingles like popping candy in his chest.

Miłosz walks up to them and sets the art supplies beside them on the stage. Things start to fall, and both teachers reach to settle them. Hands brush.

A strange sensation swoops through Miłosz's stomach. It feels like moths, biting at the fabric lining his insides and leaving him ill. This single moment, of his paint-stained hand against their dusty one, is the moment in which Miłosz's plan collapses completely.

Perhaps, if he's finally being honest with himself, the foundation had been shaky from the start.

He yanks his hand away so fast that everything topples to the floor. All he can do is stare in embarrassed horror as paper and paint slide down in a pile.

Which is more embarrassing: the sudden feelings realization with Mx. Zhéng *right there* or the immediate blunder while still reeling? Miłosz is too lost in it to decide.

"Are you alright?"

Mx. Zhéng jumps down to pick things up while Miłosz is a statue. As the seconds pass, the concern on their face grows, but Miłosz is frozen.

They put everything back on the stage, steadily this time. When they reach out for Miłosz's shoulder, he snaps out of the haze with a flinch.

Mortified.

"I am so sorry." The words fall out as a croak. His hands flutter around in search of something to do, a way to fix things, but the supplies have already been tidied. The only evidence of his mess is the distress on both their faces.

Miłosz isn't prepared for this. He hasn't had a crush since fifth grade when a classmate gave a glowing review of his art project. After realizing a few months later that he's transgender, Miłosz decided that keeping anyone and everyone at arm's length for the foreseeable future was for the best.

Apparently, the foreseeable future has ended.

"Sorry," he says again, dropping his arms limply to his sides. He's a doll with cut strings. "Actually, I'm not feeling well. We can try again tomorrow."

With that, he flees like a coward.

There's no space to process these feelings with the other teacher close enough to touch. They nearly put a hand on his shoulder, the steadying weight of an anchor pulling him down to drown.

A vent session with his dziadzio will help him work through this enough to be a person at work tomorrow instead of a walking disaster. Dziadzio knows how to cast light on things in a way that shifts the perspective into something decipherable.

He just needs to get out of here first.

There's no vent session that night, or any other night that week, because while Miłosz was tripping over a cute coworker, his dziadzio took a turn for the worse.

Nothing unexpected, the nurse assures him, but sooner than they thought. A timeline sped up with nothing to blame. It's harder when no one and nothing is at fault, because there is nowhere to direct this sticky black anger at.

With nowhere else for it to go, that anger eats him up.

Miłosz *loves* his dziadzio. Would do anything for him. Moved back to this broken ribcage of a town without hesitation for him. Miłosz will rot his soul watching dziadzio wither away if it means this man won't die alone.

Dziadzio gave up the rest of their family to stand by Miłosz when he came out as trans. Even while flirting with his deathbed, they won't come. Miłosz hates them more for this than anything they've ever done to him personally.

Not that there's anything they could do. Showing up would probably make things worse, but at least it would prove they care.

They don't, though, so it's just Miłosz crying at his dziadzio's bedside. Alone.

Miłosz takes the rest of the week off work to get things sorted.

## CANDY APPLES

Even with a round-the-clock nurse, dziadzio can't stay at home anymore. The level of care he needs can only come from a care home or a fleet of at-home medical staff they can't afford.

A care home is the only real option. For some reason, Miłosz is the only one upset about the change. "This home was always meant for you," his dziadzio writes with a shaky hand. As if this house wasn't a home only because he was here. Without him, it's just a building with soft rugs and drafty windows.

They move his dziadzio into the care home with little fanfare. The hardest part is choosing what to bring: "It's all for you," the old man writes, giving up a lifetime of belongings in a moment. A few of Miłosz's paintings to decorate the dreary walls are all he takes. The rest is left behind to haunt Miłosz in an empty house.

The first night, he can't sleep at all. The second, he sleeps fitfully and hardly at all, just enough to get through the motions of the next day and pretend everything is fine during visiting hours. By the third night, he's given up trying and spends the late hours cataloging the evidence of his grief. The next few days are much the same.

He returns to work a ghost.

## *Chapter Four*

All of Miłosz's classes are behind on the curriculum. Apparently, the substitute brought in during his emergency leave thought art classes were free time and not *actual* classes. They completely disregarded the lesson plans Miłosz scrambled to write up on that first, terrifying night.

Just another haphazard brick thrown onto his drooping shoulders.

With everything else going on, he has no capacity to even think about last week's emotional turmoil. It doesn't come to mind once until lunchtime when his usual gaggle of art students comes by for a peaceful space to eat. He musters up a smile and leaves them to their own devices.

Then Babelyn comes in.

"Are you okay?" they ask, forgoing formalities. The bluntness is something Miłosz appreciates, as little as he wants to answer the question. "You were gone all week after totally running out on Z. We were worried."

Miłosz wants to feel bad, and his heart struggles out a little zing of regret, but it's all he can manage. "I'll be fine." The truth, maybe. Hopefully.

Babelyn makes a face like they don't believe him. "Z thought maybe they did something to scare you off."

The thought freezes Miłosz on the spot. He hasn't thought about Mx. Zhéng once since he returned from his embarrassing performance in front of the other teacher. The sight of his dziadzio's friends, frantic as the nurse flittered around, put anything else from his mind.

The timeline has been sped up. An estimate of one to two years is now hopeful of half. One year, if lucky; a few months if not.

Miłosz's contract is probationary, to be revised at the end of the school year.

"My absence has nothing to do with them," Miłosz says, voice cool and neutral. It's a tone of detached professionalism perfected for difficult meetings. "However, please inform them that I will no longer be able to assist with their project. The supplies I left the other day should be intuitive enough to figure out without guidance."

He turns away in a clear dismissal. This isn't who Miłosz is, the kind of teacher he wants to be, but he is tired. He is so, *so* tired.

"Okay."

That's all. No fight, which he had expected from the firecracker. No quest for answers with prying questions or leading statements. Just acceptance.

It's enough to make him look.

"Okay," they say again, firmer this time. They're standing as tall as their 4'11 frame will let them. "I don't know what you're dealing with, but we're here if there's anything we can do."

They pause, probably hoping for a reply he can't give. With a floppy-sleeved wave as a parting gift, they leave.

If only the other students who witnessed this conversation would stop staring, then maybe Miłosz would stop feeling so seen.

Miłosz half-expects a certain coworker of his to visit at the end of the day, but they don't. Or at least they don't in the ten minutes past the final bell when Miłosz is packing up to leave. Then he's gone, off campus almost an hour earlier than usual.

Visiting hours at the care home end at seven, and he's determined to get a few hours of quality time in. Tomorrow, guests will be visiting, and it will be the first time since coming to town that they've gone a full day without seeing each other.

"You would say I'm self-sabotaging again," Miłosz confesses into the quiet. There's a tiny cup of ice cream, courtesy of a kind-eyed nurse old enough to be a patient herself, melting in his hand. "I know I am, but I feel like I have to. Isn't losing you enough? Why should I set myself up for more grief when I'm already buried in it?"

There's been no time, no space in his brain to talk about any ongoings at work. An opening upon his arrival, of course, when a note in chicken scratch asked how going back to work went. Miłosz didn't have the words to explain it then.

Or maybe he's just a coward. He seems to have plenty of words now that the person he's afraid of hearing them is asleep.

"I was going to try, I promise. Babelyn, a shared student of ours, can vouch that I marched up to the auditorium and froze like a rabbit." Miłosz chuckles, a soft, sad thing. The white rabbit is always running out of time. "I'm so afraid of being left behind, but I don't want to do the leaving either."

Figuratively, he means, because he never intended to stay. Despite his dziadzio, despite the home and lifetime of tangible memories entrusted to him, this place isn't his home. He doesn't know how to let it be.

At the start of this, when dziadzio first fell ill and Miłosz settled into this early grave of a town, he had such conviction. He was certain that he'd leave once the only person who cared for him was gone.

Now that resolve has crumbled, weak paper under watercolor paint. He should leave—still wants to; this town has always been a ghost to him. Leaving may haunt him all the same.

None of this is said once the man wakes up. Miłosz's one-sided conversation shifts to chatter about the upcoming Halloween event at school. Focusing on the staff-wide email this morning had been a struggle, but he drags up details about it, knowing dziadzio would appreciate the levity. It's not something they have much of these days.

## ALEKSANDER E. PETIT

Halloween is on the long list of things that Miłosz's mother always held a disdain for. It's too fanciful, or gaudy, or garish. Outright perverse, she would say upon seeing a costume or decoration she particularly hated. Her children were never allowed to participate in something so uncouth.

Which is why the kids were sent to their dziadzio's on that day. The mother got a break from the children, and the children got to celebrate with their mother none the wiser.

They learned how to keep secrets early in that family.

"Please let people in. It hurts to know you will be alone when I leave you."

The note, scrawled on a piece of notebook paper, is torn out and pressed into Miłosz's hands as visiting hours end. The parting blow leaves him short of breath.

Dziadzio watches, waiting for an answer Miłosz can't give. It's becoming a recurring theme in his life. *I'm afraid of getting hurt*, he can't say. *Losing you will damage me in a way I doubt I'll ever recover from*, he keeps to himself.

"I can't promise anything."

It's the only honest thing he can say.

## CANDY APPLES

When he returns to the empty house, Miłosz rereads the email. In two days' time, when he visits again, he'll need something to say.

Halloween is on a school day. The fifteen-minute homeroom period at the start of the day will be set aside for students to wander around and collect treats. Teachers are required to participate, and they must RSVP whether they'll be offering their own treats or want the cheap mix that the school is ordering in bulk. While they're obligated to hand things out, they are *not* obligated to decorate.

As an art teacher, Miłosz feels like he should. Maybe it's something he and dziadzio could plan together. The boxes of decorations in the attic of this empty house might go to waste otherwise.

He wonders if the holiday went uncelebrated while he was away at school and during his first failed year of teaching.

This will probably be their last Halloween together.

The realization squeezes like a vice on his ribcage. Tears well up in his eyes, obscuring the email and its ridiculous themed clip art.

He will definitely decorate, then. Not at the house, this wound is far too fresh for that, but at school.

The art room will be the most fanciful, gaudy, garish thing this school has ever seen outside of a play.

The next day is unsettlingly normal.

Miłosz goes to school, teaches his classes, avoids the teachers' lounge like any other day. It should be grounding, but it makes his bones itch. Normalcy feels *wrong*.

But that's how life goes, isn't it? The Earth keeps spinning no matter what happens in your little plastic imitation globe.

He thinks about going home at the end of the day. There is a house full of ghosts waiting for him with open arms.

Instead, he pulls out the ruined landscape from weeks ago. The mockery of his childhood home stirs up something long since forgotten.

Rage.

The canvas doesn't break when he throws it across the room. It's too sturdy. But it doesn't stand a chance against the box cutter from his desk. The material pulls away in jagged strips and flutters to the ground with a delicacy that makes a scream well up in his throat.

Screaming, raising his voice at all, is something Miłosz rarely considers. Silence belongs to him in a way that noise never has.

The noise forcing its way out of his throat now is strangled.

"Are you hurt?"

## CANDY APPLES

Miłosz turns so fast that he nearly topples. The box cutter slips in his hand and catches his fingers.

"Shit," the voice hisses. Footsteps draw closer, but Miłosz can't pull his gaze from the mess on the floor.

Strips of canvas pulled from its frame. Splatters of blood like raindrops. The box cutter sitting at his feet, aimed towards the voice like a compass pointing North.

The first sob hurts the most.

The rest come easier once he's given up and lowered himself to the ground.

Miłosz is so tired. He doesn't have it in him to pretend that everything is normal when nothing is okay.

"I'm here," the voice from before says, closer this time. It's familiar if Miłosz focuses on it. He doesn't. "You'll be okay. Whatever it is, you'll be okay."

There's a long while before Miłosz comes back to himself. Listening to the voice helps. Realizing that his hand is bleeding sluggishly does not.

"Oh."

Off to the side, paper tears and water runs. Something warm and damp brushes against his hand, and he jerks away.

"For your cuts."

Miłosz finally looks away from the mess of his own making and, oh, of course it's them; Nobody else would treat Miłosz with such care.

Mx. Zhéng is holding out a dampened paper towel, crouched close by but not quite touching. Their smile is valiantly holding on against the concern in their eyes.

He takes the paper towels. They rub abrasively against the cuts but wipe away most of the ugliness. Nothing a handful of bandages can't fix.

"My dziadzio, my grandfather... He's dying."

It feels more real now that he's said it out loud. Of course he's *known*, but Miłosz has always been better at evasion than denial. Don't think too hard about it, and you can't get hurt. Much. Looking at the edge of the sun hurts less than staring directly into it.

*"It hurts to know you will be alone when I leave you."*

Is that really what Miłosz wants to leave his dziadzio with: another in a long list of hurts?

"That's why I moved back here. Not to take care of him, he's had a nurse for a while, but so he won't be alone. So I won't be alone, either, for however long he has left. I don't know if I'll stay after that or leave once our time is up."

The silence that falls over them isn't the comfort Miłosz has known. The only noise is the scuff of shoes as Mx. Zhéng folds down onto the floor and tearing as Miłosz peels drying paper towel from stinging fingers.

Mx. Zhéng is the one brave enough to break the fragile stillness. "You don't have to tell me about it, and I won't try to convince you of anything. You know where to find me if that is what you want, but I won't force anything."

Their words are sweet. Respectful. They should make Miłosz's chest feel warm with care.

The lingering embers of rage grab that warmth and twist it into a *spark*.

"You've been forcing things since I started here!" It's not true, Miłosz knows that it isn't, but he can't stop now that the flames have started licking their way through his lips. "Trying to bully me into being your friend through brute force when obviously all I wanted was to be left alone. I'm not like you; I *chose* this!"

Something cracks. It takes a moment for Miłosz to realize that it's nothing tangible, no cracked ceramic or fractured glass to mend.

He glances at Mx. Zhéng and chokes down the regret pushing up his throat like bile.

"That wasn't fair of me."

"No," Mx. Zhéng agrees, face and voice crumbling in on themselves. "It was not."

They stand and brush off their pants. Shreds of glitter, a plague to the art room, fall like teardrops. Somehow it feels worse than if they'd actually cried.

There's a truth in this moment that Miłosz can't deny; if he lets Mx. Zhéng walk away now, it's over. He'll have won his solitude. It would be an empty victory, yes, but he'll have gotten what he wanted in the first place.

Except that was never the truth in the first place, was it? This is.

"You're going to walk out that door and not come back."

Mx. Zhéng stares long at the exit. Their expression is pulled tight like they're making a decision they don't want. "I am."

Unless Miłosz does something that makes a difference. Just because he's hurting doesn't give him an excuse to lash out at someone who, inexplicably, *cares*. He's losing something he didn't even have yet.

"The color of green reminds me of home." It's barely anything, certainly not enough, but it makes them pause. "Apples are my favorite food, but the ones here don't taste the same. Sometimes I wonder if I just can't tell because the memory is so old now, but dziadzio agrees."

The rest catches in his throat. He isn't ready to face it, but that doesn't matter, because it's already facing him with a blue cardigan and dark eyes.

"He doesn't want me to be alone once he goes, but I'm afraid of losing anyone else. I'm a coward, and I know it."

The world blurs out. Miłosz chokes down a sob. This is a horrible way for things to come out, the most self-sabotaging way possible. If he'd been braver, maybe things wouldn't have ended like this. Because this *is* an ending, in one way or another.

"You're not a coward." The source of the voice blurs into everything else, a swath of black and blue like a bruise. It drops to the floor in front of him and settles. "You're human."

# Chapter Five

The pair moves to a table, first aid kit in hand. Miłosz digs the lens cloth from his desk drawer to wipe his glasses, but there's still plenty for the two of them to clear up.

"Can you tell me about him? Your grandfather."

There are so many possible things to lead with, and Miłosz blurts out, "He lied to my mother *all* the time."

As an introduction, it's a great hook, albeit a bit concerning out of context.

"She had this obsession with molding me into the perfect daughter. He's the one who taught me that I didn't have to be what she wanted, and he gave me space to choose for myself who I would be. He lied to her about everything: what I did, the things I ate, why he 'had to' cut my hair when I was fourteen. Everyone else, my father and siblings, let it all happen, but he refused to let life happen *at* me."

It's a lot, he knows. Definitely more than he meant to say. Mx. Zhéng listens kindly, though, as they bandage his hands.

Miłosz tells them about a lifetime of Halloweens, whispered plans and candied apples. The holiday lost its shine for his siblings after a few years, and they stopped visiting, although they never spilled the secret. Miłosz only stopped once he left for college, and even then, he always sent a handmade card.

"This year, he's in a care home, and next year will probably be my first Halloween without him. My entire life, he's been there, and then he won't be. What am I supposed to do with that?"

Mx. Zhéng sets aside the first aid kit. One of their hands hovers over his, uncertain, but ultimately falls to the side. "Do you want advice or just a listening ear?"

The offer of advice, the suggestion of a way to move forward when he feels at a standstill, makes Miłosz's heart soar. "Advice, please."

"Build traditions. Take everything you've loved about spending the holiday with him and keep it alive. That sounds like the kind of legacy he wants to leave for you."

The longer Miłosz chews on the thought, the richer it tastes. Dziadzio has spent decades nourishing a garden in the ruins of Miłosz's life, and it would be cruel to let that rot.

Miłosz keeps worrying about being left behind, but he hardly thinks of what the man is leaving behind *for him*. Years of memories, a sense of self, a literal *home* that may not have been the first but could very well be the last. Not in the way of an anchor like he's been thinking, but a lifeboat.

Perhaps one with room for two, because the reality of things has been nipping at Miłosz's heels since he met this charming, thoughtful, determined drama teacher; Miłosz doesn't really want to drown alone on a sinking ship. And, even more than that, he wants to be not alone *with them*.

## CANDY APPLES

"Can you help me?" Miłosz pauses, realizing how large a confession that sounds. One he isn't ready for or even sure of. "With decorating my classroom, I mean. It seems like a good start."

Miłosz takes another chance, hopefully one in a future of many, and prays his hand isn't too clammy when it nests against Mx. Zhéng's.

The reaction is slow as they watch the hand move, then fall. A widening of the eyes, a gentle inhale, and the softening of it all into a precious little smile. The kind of contentedness that Miłosz would love to catch in paint on canvas.

But not today. He's only barely decided to let them into his life; the heart is off-limits.

They don't start immediately. Miłosz wants to talk to his dziadzio first, ask about borrowing some of the decorations that were a staple throughout Miłosz's childhood. Come up with some sort of plan before diving in headfirst.

The teachers don't see each other at all the next day, to Miłosz's surprise, and he leaves for the care home feeling strangely empty.

As always, he's greeted with a weak smile and a wave. The eyes are where dziadzio's joy is held, warm and brown and bright.

"Hey, dziadziu." Miłosz lowers himself gently into the chair reserved for him five days of the week. "I have an update you might like."

He doesn't detail all of it, the moth-eaten feeling of being seen or lingering indecision of where to go next, but he hits the finer points. There is finally someone he's willing to let in, and this person will be helping him decorate for Halloween.

The next few hours are lighter than any since dziadzio moved here. They laugh, and they smile, and none of it is forced.

By the time visiting hours are over, Miłosz has a very loose concept and firm instructions not to come back until he's inventoried the boxes of decorations at home.

He tries his hardest to think of the place as that, even though it feels wrong.

Saturday morning is spent refining their plans, deciding what can be used or repurposed, what could be made from scratch to match it.

In years past, dziadzio made things silly and whimsical so as not to frighten his grandchildren. Fun and palatable, although with no set theme. Miłosz, in a moment of dark humor and grief, decides that their final Halloween should be themed after all.

"It's something a student said," he explains, reworking their notes in a Halloween-appropriate purple pen. "They will enjoy it, if nobody else."

That's enough to make dziadzio laugh despite the underlying sadness in his eyes.

"It will be amazing," the man agrees in violet ink, and it means more to Miłosz than anything.

They have a battle plan ready to present by Monday. Miłosz clutches the messily-filled notebook close to his heart as he steps out of his classroom at the end of the day.

Only to walk directly into someone's chest.

Miłosz staggers back, nearly tripping over his own feet, and stops when an arm in a familiar cardigan catches him.

"Are you alright?"

"You ask that a lot." It's not what he meant to say, and a dusting of blush sputters across his cheeks. "I'm fine. Thank you for catching me."

"Any time." They sport their own blush, which Miłosz tries to ignore. Realizing that their hand still rests on his hip isn't any better. It's intimate.

Distracting.

"May I help you?" While Miłosz would like to think they had the same plan as him, to have a tactical holiday meeting, he could never assume for fear of being made a fool.

Mx. Zhéng pulls their hand away. It brushes slowly, lingeringly, along his side. "I wanted to see how you're doing and ask if you still want help decorating."

They're on the same page, then. Wonderful. Miłosz lets out a soft little sigh of relief that he hopes the other doesn't notice.

He takes a step back, carefully this time, and turns into the classroom. He'll be more comfortable laying things out in his own space anyway; It'll let him point out where he would like things to go.

"I was going to bring this over to you." He gestures with the notebook before setting it on a table and crowding around it. The pages, when he flips through them, are smeared and stained with inky purple ramblings.

It feels like sharing a piece of himself. This is something he and his dziadzio poured their hearts into, an overflowing, fragile cup. His past, present, and future are laid out in these scribbles.

"There are a few things I'll have to make by hand or repurpose, but I can accomplish a lot with what's available. The most difficult part will likely be the costume."

Mx. Zhéng walks up behind him, close enough to nearly touch, and reaches tentatively for the notebook. Miłosz lets them page through it while he vehemently ignores the proximity. It's something he's never had an opportunity to get used to.

It's odd to think that now he might.

"You'll be wearing this?" they ask, dreadfully close to Miłosz's ear.

"Theoretically, if I can find the pieces," he forces out through gritted teeth. "Could you stand back, please?"

They tilt their head to look at Miłosz's face. This close, their nose brushes his cheek.

"Oh," they breathe. "Sorry."

Miłosz waits, breath held, but they don't move. "Is that a no?"

"Oh!" This time, they step back. "Sorry."

It's hard to ignore the flush across Mx. Zhéng's cheeks, but Miłosz is stubborn. He trains his gaze on the notebook without straying to the hands holding it. "I plan to visit the local thrift stores tomorrow afternoon in search of costume pieces."

"I could..." The words stall and sputter out.

"You could?" Miłosz asks, convincing himself to look up.

The other teacher seems conflicted but ultimately lets their shoulders drop. "I could also dress up," they say, words dripping with a lie that Miłosz can't place, "but I don't know what I'd wear."

There's silence while Miłosz struggles to find the untruth. Then it clicks into place with a click of Miłosz's tongue.

"That's not what you were going to say, was it?"

"No," they confess. Their attempt at a smile is flimsy. "But I don't want to push."

Miłosz realizes something horrible and important between those lines: he never apologized for the barbed words he lashed out with last week. He admitted that it was unfair, but he didn't own up to it. Mx. Zhéng deserves at least that much.

Reaching out has never been easy for Miłosz, but he does it now. The notebook slips easily from Mx. Zhéng's fingers when tugged. It's set aside for Miłosz's hands to fill the space.

"I'm sorry. What I said was cruel. You've been respectful of every boundary I've set. If anything, I'm the one giving mixed signals. While it's no excuse for my behavior, I hope you understand the reason for it."

With a gentle squeeze, Miłosz looks away and rounds out his apology. While he was able to look into Mx. Zhéng's eyes for the rest, he can't do it for this. "You were hurt, and it wasn't fair to you. I will try my best not to hurt you again in the future, but I can't promise it. My best attempt is all I can offer."

A grain of truth in his thorned words the other day was that Miłosz is a solitary creature. Up until now, he's *chosen* to be alone. It was always safer, more comfortable. He found solace in it. But he doesn't think he's ever hurt somebody with it before.

He doesn't like the monster that grief has made him.

Guessing what they had meant to say earlier, Miłosz takes a risk. It's one that Mx. Zhéng has already taken several times over. "If you're available tomorrow, would you like to join me?"

The hand in his squeezes back. "You don't have to offer, it's alright."

"I *want* you to come with me. If it's not a burden."

"Then I'd love to."

## CANDY APPLES

They stand there for a while like that, practically holding hands. Miłosz stares anywhere but at his companion and tries not to wonder where they're looking. If they might be looking at him.

# *Chapter Six*

Miłosz isn't ready to be a person with someone else. He hasn't interacted socially with anyone in years, sticking to routines and scripts. The craving was never there until this endlessly kind theater teacher walked into his life.

Sometimes, Miłosz wonders if that poster project of theirs was just an excuse to start a conversation. Every once in a while, Miłosz is weak enough to let himself believe that it's true.

They meet in Miłosz's classroom at the end of the day. There's still paint in his hair, on his cheek, spilt between his fingers from when a student upended their palette onto him at the end of class.

"Rough day?"

Miłosz closes his eyes tight and takes a deep breath to push down the embarrassment of being seen like this: more paint-splattered than usual, cleaning the mess on his hands and knees, but ultimately just smearing it because the school refuses to buy proper cleaning supplies. There will be soapy stains along the shins of these pants until the end of time.

"Just an accident. The student almost missed his bus while apologizing so much, but I assured him that I could clean up on my own. I may need to stop briefly for a change of clothes before we head to the shops, though."

He gathers up the sopping pile of paper towels and gingerly dumps it in the nearest trash can. His fingers are tacky, and the color stains even once he shoves his hands in the sink.

"We could meet up at the store if that's easier for you. I wouldn't mind."

It *would* be easier, but Miłosz is striving not to always take the easy route.

They talked about it last night, he and his dziadzio. After leaving Mx. Zhéng with the notebook to peruse, Miłosz went to visit the care home only slightly later than usual. The pride on dziadzio's face made every awkward, flush-cheeked moment worth it. For the first time in a while, he knew he was doing the *right* thing instead of the *comfortable* one.

"If you don't mind waiting while I get ready, we can go together. I live five minutes away and shouldn't take long."

Inviting the other teacher to his house is a much bigger step than he'd intended to take today. It's hard to regret it, though, when he turns to grab dry paper towels and sees Mx. Zhéng's wide grin over his shoulder.

"That would be great. I don't mind waiting.

Miłosz dries his hands, packs up his satchel bag, and they head out to the parking lot.

His clunker of a run-red four-door groans when they open the doors and growls upon starting. The air freshener is brand new and scents the space overwhelmingly with fake apple blossoms.

There's a classic yellow rubber duck homed in the otherwise empty ashtray.

Miłosz loves his shitty car.

The drive is quick, made even quicker by Mx. Zhéng's comments. They like the duck. They don't drive or have a car, but at home they have a collection of scented candles. They enjoy ocean scents, but they don't specify why, if there even *is* a reason.

The steering wheel creaks in Miłosz's grip as they approach the house. It's a squat thing with low ceilings and paint in desperate need of a touch-up. The mailbox was handmade well over two decades ago, when they first moved, but it still stands tall. The ramp added last year needs to be swept clear of crunching leaves.

"This is my home," Miłosz says, trying to convince himself more than his companion.

"Should I wait out here or come in?"

Miłosz appreciates the out, but they've already come this far. "You can come in."

Like the art room, Miłosz hasn't changed anything. Couldn't bring himself to do it even if he wanted, which he does not. The collection of tchotchkes, photographs, and secondhand furniture is a familiar comfort.

The front door opens directly into the living room. He waves a hand at the jumble of mismatched furniture. "Make yourself comfortable. I'll be right back."

They're going to look at the photos, he knows. It's hard not to feel uncomfortable with being seen pre-transition by someone who only knows him as he is now. All he can do is trust that they'll be gentle with the knowledge.

Without professionalism to worry about, Miłosz dresses for himself. A soft maroon tee shirt under a light jacket, jeans so loved that the knees and thighs are nearly worn through, boots that give him the posture and confidence to stand taller.

As he passes by his dresser on the way out of his room, he pauses. Puts a finishing touch on his outfit. Sees his smile in the mirror and doesn't flinch.

"I'm ready," he calls softly into the living room.

Mx. Zhéng stands exactly where Miłosz had expected: directly in front of the photo wall. They turn in a rush with guilt threaded through their eyes. "I'm sorry, I didn't mean to snoop."

Miłosz shrugs, trying to show off a calm he doesn't feel. "I wouldn't have invited you in if I minded." He approaches the wall and points to a specific photo with a smile. "This one was right after I came out to him. It was years before I told anyone else."

It's not a spectacular photo. He's caught halfway in a squint, and everything is blurry because they messed up the timer. But Miłosz sports a fresh—if horribly messy and obviously done at home by a shaky old man's hand—haircut and hand-me-down slacks. This was the first in a long line of truly happy photos, all laid out on this wall.

"Wait a second." Mx. Zhéng's gaze falls on a particular photo, and Miłosz fights back a blush at the ribbing he knows is coming. "You never mentioned being in theater!"

"Technically, I wasn't."

His predecessor had helped the previous theater teachers out much like this one, offering feedback or a helping hand. Miłosz wasn't a particularly social child, so he often had a spare hand or two. Painting set pieces had filled many of his senior year lunch periods as a distraction from his fractured home life, and the theater teacher insisted that he be included in the group photo for their spring show. In the picture, Miłosz is spotted with paint and smiling nervously, much like the photo on his current work ID.

"You're in the photo, though!"

"I painted sets. I never even interacted with most of the cast or crew." That's mostly true, aside from the stagehand who tried to flirt with him all the time. It was horribly uncomfortable and mostly just awkward. "One crew member kept asking me out, but I wasn't interested. That's the extent of my interactions."

"Have you ever been interested?" they ask, still staring at the photo. "In dating, I mean."

Miłosz shrugs and tries not to read into it. "You know me," he says, feeling almost giddy with it. When's the last time someone *knew* him? "I've never really been the type to get close to people, and I can't imagine entering a relationship with someone I don't know well."

Out of the corner of his eye, Miłosz steals a glance at Mx. Zhéng. They're staring so firmly at the photo that Miłosz wonders if they're avoiding looking somewhere else.

"Is there something wrong with my outfit? Or did I miss some paint?" He probably did, but paint splotches are a staple of his daily look at this point. "If I look weird, you can tell me."

Their gaze snaps to his, dark eyes meeting light. "Not weird, I'm just not used to seeing you outside of work clothes."

Miłosz will not be touching that statement with a ten-foot pole.

"You look nice," they promise, expression melting into a familiar smile. "I didn't know you wear jewelry."

Most of the time, he doesn't. His fingers drift up to the dainty silver chain loose around his neck. From it dangles a tiny enamel apple in stark cherry red.

"I like apples."

As a child, he was fixated on the tiny orchid tucked in the corner of dziadzio's farm. Most of his days were spent in the low branches of trees. In middle school, his class took a field trip to an apple orchard, and he got in trouble for trying to climb a tree.

He stopped wearing earrings years ago, but the matching pair still lives on his dresser.

"I'm ready to go if you are."

They leave without any further awkwardness and pile back into the car. Their first stop, a dingy little secondhand shop that focuses mainly on clothing, holds the most promise.

It's also, unfortunately, crowded. The tall racks and shelves make it easy to get lost. Miłosz is average height at best, and Mx. Zhéng only has a few inches on him,

There's a simple solution, and Miłosz only has a moment to consider it before Mx. Zhéng starts to disappear around a corner.

He shoots out an arm, quick to grab their fingers. They stop and turn back, expression startled.

"We were about to get separated."

The fingers curl, trapping them together. Despite that being the intention, it makes Miłosz's hands clammy and ribs itch. He doesn't dare pull away.

They walk around the shop like that, fingers intertwined except for when they need to inspect an article of clothing. As soon as it goes back onto the rack or into their basket, Mx. Zhéng ties them back together.

The longer it goes on, the sweatier his hands and drier his throat get. He wipes his hands on the thighs of his jeans at any available opportunity.

At the end of history's slowest, most agonizing hour, they walk out with a few gems. But it's not enough, so they move on to the next shop. Miłosz can't decide if it's a curse or a mercy that this one is less crowded. There's no reason for Mx. Zhéng to reach over and take his hand again.

Except they do it again anyway.

"Mx. Zhéng?"

They smile, as they always do, and run their thumb across Miłosz's knuckles. He stops breathing. "We're not at school, you know. You can call me Tāo if you want."

Miłosz isn't sure he *does* want that. Only a few days have passed since deciding to let his guard down, and the other teacher has taken it as an invitation to swing a sledgehammer around. Walls he hadn't meant to sacrifice were demolished in the crossfire, and he's the one who tore down the first brick. Letting himself be vulnerable is *exhausting*.

He turns away from that charming grin and dives into the nearest rack of clothing, all the while holding on.

These feelings aren't something he's willing to acknowledge yet. For now, though, he can still appreciate the company of the fluttering moths around his heart.

# *Chapter Seven*

"I have no idea what to do with them! They've been nothing but kind and respectful to an infuriating degree!"

Miłosz talks with his hands, careful to give his dziadzio a safe amount of space. One cup had already been knocked to the ground, and they're trying to avoid a repeat.

"How can they be so overwhelming with so little? I set the boundaries myself, and it still feels like a toed line."

After making the mistake of mentioning Mx. Zhéng the other day, they're all dziadzio asks about. But it's okay because they're all Miłosz can *think* about aside from the looming weight of the holiday. It's hard to think of one without his mind wandering to the other.

"I just don't understand–" Miłosz cuts off his tirade when he realizes that he's not sure what to say. What *doesn't* he understand? Why Mx. Zhéng would have any interest in the brooding art teacher in the first place? Or why Miłosz, brooding as he is, would not only allow but *accept* it? Or maybe the fact that he's slowly inching towards *joy* of all things during what should be a horrible period of his life. And it is, of course it is, but he hadn't thought it could be more than that.

## CANDY APPLES

Wrinkled hands reach for a pen and notepad. The pages are slightly damp and water-stained from the water glass incident.

His handwriting has been getting worse. Soon enough, Miłosz's familiarity with it will be the only way to decipher the scribbles.

"It is alright to love and be loved."

The word, even written, makes Miłosz's chest ache.

"What about you? All the photos of babunia are at home; you didn't bring any."

Dziadzio simply smiles. There's an uncharacteristic steadiness in his hand as he writes. "I remember her clearly as the day we met. You need the reminder."

That particular truth is an old, dull ache, like how the memory of his childhood home blurs into shades of green without a photograph to distinguish the shape.

His babunia passed when he was too young to remember her well, and he only has two memories with any clarity. They're both soft around the edges with age but distinct.

The first is baking apple pies together. He was too small at that age to reach the counter, so she sat him on top of it. With a basket of apples in his lap and a peeler in hand, she walked him through the recipe. Most of the details are long gone, and she never wrote them down. Miłosz asked dziadzio to help him recreate it not long after moving to the United States, nostalgic for a taste of home, but he didn't know the recipe either.

The second memory sits on his dresser with unworn earrings. The crochet doll, lovingly handmade in a now-faded candy-apple red, was shaped like an apple dinosaur to humor a young child's interests, and it long outlived its creator. Babunia may not have been able to watch Miłosz grow up, but this part of her has.

It's easier to think of things in that light with someone he barely remembers. The loss is still there, but the full force of devastation doesn't hit for an echo.

*Anything you put love into will shine*, babunia always said. Her voice is lost to him, the way she said the words, but the heart in them is as clear as the feel of Cardamom's yarn.

Miłosz loves Halloweens spent handing out candy on his dziadzio's porch. He loves game nights that always inevitably devolve into throwing cards at each other over cheating accusations. He loves standing side-by-side in the kitchen, under the small rays of sunlight that sneak in through the window over the sink. He *loves*.

It's a lot to face losing, and he doesn't know how to hold on.

Balancing Halloween preparation with care home visits and lesson plans leaves Miłosz feeling pulled like taffy, spread thin but stubbornly holding together.

There's a sense of melancholy souring any joy he finds. And he is finding it, much to his surprise.

Dziadzio is delighted.

# CANDY APPLES

Miłosz is conflicted.

Mx. Zhéng is caught in the center of it all.

"Are you alright?" That question again, the one that makes him want to peel away his skin and dissolve.

"Please," Miłosz emphasizes, setting down the prop flowers in his hands before he does something stupid and destructive, "*please*, stop asking me that."

The answer is no. The answer is yes. The answer is that Miłosz is experiencing loss and joy in a slow-motion collision that will take both of them as casualties.

The answer is that, every time Mx. Zhéng shows care towards Miłosz, it gets harder to breathe.

"Alright." The reply is gentle, as always. They never push.

Sometimes Miłosz wants to. He wonders what changed him to become like this: the impending loss of one person or the looming gain of someone else.

A knock pulls them away from the flowers and what sits in the silence between them. Miłosz allows himself a grounding breath before turning to the door.

"Hey, guys!" Already Miłosz is grimacing. The school's secretary, whose name Miłosz can't remember for the life of him, leans leisurely against the doorframe. He looks out of place in white dress pants that wouldn't survive a minute in the art room. "I'm placing the bulk candy order for Halloween, and you're the only one who hasn't RSVP'd, Mr. Jagoda."

"I'll be making my own, so that won't be necessary. Thank you."

The man blinks, wide-eyed and owlish, for an uncomfortable minute. "I see. Carry on then." He's gone in the next moment, and Miłosz could not be more glad for it.

"What are you planning to make?" Mx. Zhéng's hands have returned to the flowers. The colors are poisonously bright against their pale skin. "If you don't mind my asking."

"An old family recipe." Unlike the apple pie, this is one he's made often enough that his hands know the routine down to the bones and tendons. "Krówki can be compared to a cream fudge, but it's typically packaged like candies."

He's already started a search for the right type of wrapper. Wax paper is used to wrap the treats, and he's hoping to find a decorative one for the holiday.

Mx. Zhéng turns their attention back to the task at hand, passing him a finished cluster of blooms. Immediately, they start on the next one. "I don't spend much time in the kitchen. I know some basics, but it never seemed worthwhile to learn without someone to cook for or with. My sister and I don't care enough about what we eat to bother."

This is the first time they've mentioned family. Miłosz latches onto the tidbit with both hands, abandoning the fake flowers. "You have a sister?"

Their hands pause. A considering look crosses their face and doesn't budge until the hands do. "Ying is living with me while she gets her master's degree. Our schedules don't line up, so we don't see each other often, and we're not very close."

Miłosz can relate. Despite growing up in the same household, raised by the same parents, he and his siblings never got along. His sister clung to their overbearing perfectionist mother, whose eyes only Miłosz inherited. His brother idolized their passive and distant father, whom Miłosz got his dark curls from. And Miłosz, the black sheep of their family, found solidarity with the only other person who never quite settled into American living.

"I've never been close with my siblings either."

They could talk about it more, but they don't. Miłosz has nothing else to say unless prompted for something specific, and he wonders if Mx. Zhéng is the same or if they're simply afraid to push. It's something Miłosz *could* offer but doesn't know how to.

The flowers are easier to focus on. Art, in any form, has always been easier for Miłosz than people.

One of the thrift stores they'd visited had a bulk assortment of fake flowers for cheap, and Miłosz filled his trunk with them. The variety of shapes and colors will work beautifully in bringing his art room wonderland to life. Each arrangement is unique, and while he could sort them all himself, it would take twice as long and be half as interesting.

"Thank you," he says, knowing it's a sentiment he doesn't express enough. Mx. Zhéng has helped Miłosz in many ways since coming into his life, and Miłosz has failed to acknowledge most of them. Some are too big to say. Others are too small to face without embarrassment. This one, at least, can fit in his mouth and fall from his tongue.

"No problem!" Mx. Zhéng's responding smile is warmer than ever, falling over him like sun rays. "I enjoy this kind of thing, and even if I didn't, the time with you would be worth it."

The blatant affection is still something Miłosz doesn't know what to do with. Powering past it without comment is the only way to protect himself until he comes to some sort of decision. Decision on what, he isn't entirely sure, because there never was a question placed.

It looms over him like a game of Hangman, and he's the man.

The longer the statement sits between them, the more Miłosz itches to say something. *Anything*. "It's a shame none of these are apple blossoms. As you might guess, those are my favorite flower. Due to liking apples, I mean."

The topic is random and meaningless in most ways, but Mx. Zhéng humors him in a way that feels more genuine than appeasing.

"Maybe we should've picked something with an apple theme then."

A snort escapes before Miłosz can catch it. An undignified trait, his mother used to say. "I don't believe Snow White would be a better option, considering the only thing we have in common is enjoying apples. Though her dress *would* be an easier costume to get ahold of. And I'm sure we could find a prince costume for you as well."

It's a slip; Miłosz knows as soon as the words leave his mouth. Not the part about calling Mx. Zhéng a prince, because Miłosz had already established the irrelevance of gender by calling himself a princess moments before. No, it was the part where he insinuated that Mx. Zhéng could be *his* prince. There's an admission in it that Miłosz has been hiding from for fear of what change it might bring.

Mx. Zhéng takes it in stride, somehow knowing the perfect thing to say. "You would be a horrible princess."

As tempted as Miłosz is to say, "You would be a wonderful prince," he doubts the sentiment would be as well-received. And it's not quite true anyway.

Sometimes, tucked into the corners of plastic smiles and a placating voice, Miłosz sees a reflection of his own childhood. Expectations you can neither meet nor escape. Mx. Zhéng hasn't spoken on it much, but it's easy to recognize the weight they share.

"It would be best to keep our theme, then. You still won't tell me your costume?"

Another smile, sharper than most in a way that captures Miłosz's breath. "No."

"Maybe this was a terrible idea."

Miłosz is by his dziadzio's bedside again, fruit cup in one hand and plastic spoon in the other. If he were home, he would pick through it with his fingers, but at the care home, he attempts to use manners.

The look dziadzio sends him is brimming with amusement. *Traitor*, Miłosz thinks, no venom behind it.

"Dziadziu, it is not funny," Miłosz pouts. "I don't have space in my life for what they're offering."

Whether he means the overtures of friendship or the thinly veiled something else that he refuses to look directly at isn't stated. Either is correct.

Miłosz is *trying* to make space in his life. It is difficult, and it is bittersweet. A lot of the time, he wonders if he's making the right choices.

When his dziadzio smiles the way he does now, it's a little easier to think so.

"I know you want me not to be alone, but would it really be so bad?" Would the hollowness of solitude be that much worse than the transparency of being seen?"

He's being daft; it's obvious in the raise of dziadzio's brows.

"Fine. But when my heart bursts the next time they hold my hand, I'm blaming you."

That's something it seems his dziadzio can live with.

Every day during lunch, a group of students comes to the art room. It's the same refuge from high school life now as it was during Miłosz's teenage years.

It's also the reason why he insists to Mx. Zhéng that eating lunch together is not an option.

"I need to keep an eye on the students," Miłosz insists, leaning into the excuse. They're in the art room after school, mapping a layout for the flower arrangements. "You would distract me."

Mx. Zhéng's face is barely visible behind the massive arrangement in their arms, but Miłosz catches the sharp edge of a grin. "That's good to know. Most of the time, I wonder if I affect you at all."

"Really?" Miłosz finds that hard to believe. Despite his best efforts, his reactions have the same subtlety as Mx. Zhéng's advances.

Their lips tilt into a smirk. "No."

With every passing day, Mx. Zhéng grows more audacious in their comfort. Miłosz tries not to bask in it.

He snorts instead, clinging to the veil of apathy that's fooling nobody. "Either way, the answer is no. We'll have to find some other opportunity for you to charm me."

Two allusions to how their amicable nature affects Miłosz in one conversation? He really *is* slipping.

The reaction is everything he expects: bright eyes, soft mouth, a joy that Miłosz himself doesn't know how to hold. "I'd love to."

That's the problem.

Ever since dziadzio used the word "love," it's been banging around his skull like a logo on a screensaver. Even if he does hold some level of affection for his coworker, it isn't love. There's an exhilarating horror in knowing that it could be if he stopped smothering the sapling in his chest.

"Next Wednesday, I'll be staying late to decorate my classroom, and afterwards, I'm going home to make my treats. You can join me if you'd like."

The number of people that Miłosz has shared a kitchen with fits on one hand. His babunia, according to faded memories. Dziadzio, of course. Classmates during a middle school home economics class, though he mostly ignored them and worked alone. Miłosz has always been more like his grandfather than anyone wanted him to be; a horrible daughter, a wonderful grandson.

"Are you sure?"

Mx. Zhéng's voice is cautious, almost brittle. A tentative out offered to a skittish animal.

Miłosz might be offended if it weren't warranted.

"You won't learn your way around a kitchen otherwise. It's a valuable skill to have."

Having someone in his space again will be scary, but Mx. Zhéng is difficult to be scared of. They've proven that Miłosz is something to be handled preciously. He might never get used to that.

## CANDY APPLES

In light of their conversation, Miłosz doesn't expect Mx. Zhéng to show up at his classroom during lunch the next day, but they do.

"I'll be out of your hair in a second," they promise. There's a tote bag hanging from one arm and a mug held by the other. Both are placed on Miłosz's desk. "Just dropping these off. Have a nice lunch!"

They're gone in the millisecond it takes Miłosz to blink.

"Open it!"

He sends a flat look to Babelyn, who's been spending more lunch periods in the art room recently. They've been quiet but clear in their worries about him. Between Babelyn and Mx. Zhéng, he hasn't felt more transparent in his life.

The package is nothing special when he opens it with careful hands: a pack of colored pencils.

"They were just returning some borrowed art supplies." Though Miłosz doesn't know why they waited; the posters were finished a while ago, according to the teacher's rambling.

Babelyn smirks. "Were they returning that drink, too?"

That part is harder to brush off. With flushed cheeks, Miłosz picks up the mug. It's warm to the touch and steaming, so it must be fresh. His first guess would be tea, but it smells richer. He takes a tentative sip.

Then immediately takes another, because this is hot apple cider and he's never been able to resist his favorite fruit.

Forget everything that Miłosz has said about Mx. Zhéng so far. Set aside the kind words, patience, the cautious hands offering comfort. *This* is the moment that changes everything.

Miłosz looks up from the drink, smile impossible to smother. He barely bothers to try.

"Could you do me a favor, Babelyn? When you see Mx. Zhéng later for class, please let them know that I've changed my mind and will be providing lunch tomorrow."

"The other day, I mentioned in passing that I like apples. Today, they brought me apple cider."

Dziadzio smiles, gestures with a raised hand for Miłosz to continue. The color in his cheeks deems it a good day.

"I've been so determined not to get attached. I'm already—" The words get stuck in his throat. He finds the strength to spit them out. "I'm already losing you, so I didn't want to latch onto anyone else I could lose. When you're gone, I might not even stay. But how can I turn away from someone who..."

Someone who respects his boundaries to the letter but finds a loophole to deliver an emotional sucker punch. Who understands not only "yes" and "no" but also "maybe." Who listens with care then acts with kindness.

Someone who nudges but never pushes.

## CANDY APPLES

There's a glint in dziadzio's eyes that Miłosz knows well, one that has followed him since he was old enough to understand it.

"Just because you can't say 'I told you so' doesn't mean I don't hear it."

The smug grin doesn't leave his face for the rest of the night.

# Chapter Eight

Choosing what to make for lunch is more difficult than Miłosz had anticipated.

Mx. Zhéng hasn't gone into detail about their dietary preferences, so Miłosz pieces together a plan based on what little he knows. The lunchbox he packs for them is light and fresh.

He includes a batch of orange shortbread cookies made last night in an attempt to settle his nerves. It may not have worked, but they're a personal touch to round out the meal.

While packing everything up, he wonders what on Earth he's doing. Is one little drink really enough to sway him so thoroughly?

*Yes*, a voice in the back of his mind, where he's a softer creature, sighs.

He bats it away and commits to a firm maybe.

The tote bag functioning as his lunchbox weighs heavily as he walks through the halls of the school. It goes into the breakroom fridge, out of sight but lingering in his mind.

The figure waiting outside his locked classroom door isn't the one he expects.

"Babelyn? What are you doing here so early?"

## CANDY APPLES

Curled up by the door, knees tucked to their chest, is Miłosz's favorite student. Their face is pressed to their knees and, for a terrifying moment, he thinks they might be crying.

But at his voice, their head shoots up. Drool trails down their chin. "Wuh?" The tired student wipes sleep from their eyes and yawns. "Oh, hey, Mr. J. I've been waiting *forever*."

Still worried, although not nearly as much, he joins them on the floor. The linoleum is chilly through his slacks. Sitting in the classroom would be more comfortable, but it's been a while since he indulged in floor time.

"What did you need me for? Especially this early. You could have come to me during class."

They uncurl, stretching legs to reveal a small bag clutched to their chest. "I got you something, and I wanted to give it to you before Z got here in case you wanted to wear it."

Wear it? Miłosz takes the gift with a mix of confusion and nerves. What if he doesn't like it? No matter what, he'll say that he does.

Babelyn ignores whatever Miłosz's face is doing and keeps talking. "I saw them at the same place I get my sunflower hairclips. Since Z said you like apples, I thought you might like these." Their head tilts in question. "Though I guess I don't know if you like wearing your hair up."

He does. Some days, the feeling of curls brushing his neck is too much, and he needs it out of the way. He just keeps losing his hair ties and forgetting to replace them.

There are two things in the bag, past the obligatory layer of tissue paper. The first is a set of scrunchies on a cardboard sheet: apple print, red with an apple slice charm, green with an apple charm, and plain off-white, like the inside of an apple. The second is a set of headbands in the same designs.

Miłosz already knows that the way to emotionally devastate him is with the thing he's cherished most since childhood, but tearing up on the hallway floor is unbecoming.

"Thank you," he whispers, voice thick. "These are brilliant."

Today, he wore a cream-colored sweater in anticipation of a quiet self-study day. It's not quite the same color as the accessories, but it's close enough. He loosens the patterned hair tie from the cardstock backing and makes his best attempt at taming unruly curls.

Miłosz holds his head a little taller.

"Thank you, really."

Babelyn ducks their head. "No problem. You're having a rough time, and I thought you could use a pick-me-up. We all do sometimes."

He hasn't explained the situation with his dziadzio in any detail; he refuses to dump that on a child. He did briefly mention that a family member is ill, and it's a difficult time for them. They accepted it with a solemn nod and handed him a glittery sunflower sticker. It lives on the nameplate at his desk.

"Besides, it's as much a gift for Z as it is for you. They're gonna melt when they see you."

## CANDY APPLES

Melt is a good way to describe the way Mx. Zhéng softens around him. The fake smiles dissolve into something sweeter, more authentic.

There's no guarantee it means something, though. They've never mentioned wanting anything other than friendship, and the steaming mug of apple cider wasn't a love letter, no matter how much it felt like one.

Miłosz is starting to think he might want it to be one.

"At the very least, it will keep my hair out of my mouth when I see them for lunch."

There's a danger in the knife-sharp way Babelyn grins. "Lunch? You really think they won't stop by before class after an invitation like that?"

They flap their hands, sleeves flopping. The oversized sweater of the day is a mossy green patterned with metallic vines. The embroidery was done by hand, if the lack of uniformity in the stitches is any indication.

"Hey, Z, Mr. J invited you over for lunch tomorrow. Yes, I'm sure. No, I'm not scheming." An eyeroll. "Yes, he was very clear, so there's no way I'm misunderstanding. And you aren't allowed to bring food. Don't even think about it. Stop thinking about it; I see you thinking about it. No."

Before Miłosz can even *think* about how to reply to all of that, the student stands and brushes dirt from their pants. "Anyway, I should go study for my math test."

"Ah, thank you. Good luck." But they're already halfway down the hall.

Interacting with Babelyn is always such a whirlwind.

The rest of the scrunchies and headbands take pride of place in the top drawer of his desk.

It's not long before there's a tentative knock on his doorframe. Soft, barely there. If Miłosz weren't half-expecting someone, he would have missed it.

Miłosz looks up from his scribbled lesson plan, and his breath catches.

Mx. Zhéng is in the doorway, handsome as ever. Their long cardigan is flat black and tantalizingly fluffy. Under it are a crisp white dress shirt and grey slacks that *must* be a different cut than usual for how they grip the thighs. Dress shoes are swapped out for low-heeled boots. Their earrings are clouds crying little blue crystal raindrops.

Breath-taking.

A wave of embarrassment floods over Miłosz as he realizes he's staring. It washes away when he finds that he's not the only one.

"Good morning," Miłosz greets, attempting some facsimile of normalcy. There's no reason to act like the heartsick teenagers they teach. "You look nice. May I help you with something?"

The other teacher shakes themself out of their stupor with a sheepish smile. "Yeah, good morning. I don't think I've ever seen you with your hair up. It looks…"

"Functional?" he offers when they flounder. He twirls a curl around a finger to help ground himself; the repetitive motion is soothing. "My hair will be out of the way for lunch."

The word seems to jolt through them. "Right! Lunch. I just wanted to confirm since you seemed pretty set on no lunches the other day."

Miłosz shrugs. Maybe if he brushes it off, they won't think too hard about it. "I've decided that I could use a distraction after all."

That's the part Miłosz is most afraid of. Mx. Zhéng has done a good job of helping Miłosz find sweetness in the bitter, but he's afraid he'll lose sight of his grief. He doesn't want to forget dziadzio's face and need a photograph to remember it.

But he doesn't want melancholy to be what he remembers of the man either.

"I do still have students to watch, so I'll grab our food from the breakroom and then meet you here. Is that alright?" The shift to a less fraught topic is hopefully smoother than it feels.

"Yeah." Their mouth is poised open as if to say more. They don't.

"Lovely. I'll see you then."

The dismissal is clear. Miłosz waits for Mx. Zhéng to go. Any minute now.

"Don't you have a class to prepare for?"

"Of course." The words are syrupy and slow. Their eyes follow as Miłosz tilts his head, ponytail swaying. Perhaps Babelyn was right about the hair after all. "Right, I'll see you later. Bye."

Finally, they turn to let Miłosz dissect this conversation in peace.

And walk face-first into the doorframe.

"I'm fine," they shout, glancing over their shoulder one last time. "Bye!"

A smothered laugh breaks out as soon as they're out of sight. Not in a mean way, but charmed.

He's looking forward to lunch more than he'd like to admit.

Babelyn spends first period bouncing in their seat. The other students cast glances that go ignored. They paint a lopsided tree spotted with sunflowers, uncaring that the flowers don't grow on trees. Everything is warm browns and yellows and greens.

Self-directed study days are a tool Miłosz uses to evaluate how much a student has learned so far during the course. As long as a student creates *something* to show they've paid attention in class, they get full credit. Seeing what ideas they come up with on their own is an adventure, and only one student needs a reminder not to paint nudity. Overall, a successful class.

The rest of the morning passes in the same way, evaluating his students' progress by giving them the freedom of their own inspirations. A gentle reminder that they're more than their ability to follow.

That was a painful lesson for Miłosz.

A lot has changed since he was a student here. Almost everything, mostly for the better. He's come a long way from the dedicated daughter mask he once wore. His mother would have never approved of the choices that led him here.

Finding Mx. Zhéng waiting in his classroom with a shy smile and a thermos, Miłosz has never been more glad to disappoint her.

"You weren't supposed to bring anything," he chides, though the smile he can't bury undermines it.

They shrug, the picture of ease. Once upon a time, Miłosz thought they were too cool for fidgeting hands to come across as nervous, but now he knows the truth; Miłosz inherited cold eyes and nervous hands, while Mx. Zhéng stores energy in the hands and emotions in the eyes.

"I wasn't sure if you liked the cider, so I brought more. I'll drink it if you don't want it."

Miłosz levels them with an unimpressed quirk of the brow. No amount of nonchalance can cover that nonsense. "You know I do."

Liking apples in any form is a fact of Miłosz and being used to gain his favor. Obviously, since they're here, it's working. Someone cared enough to *listen*; that means more than the drink itself does.

That someone is grinning unapologetically. The cuff of their cardigan frays where they fidget with it. Well-loved. "I want to know all the things you like."

The words land heavy and warm on his shoulders, a blanket of care. The weight is unfamiliar and almost uncomfortable.

Miłosz's heart squirms under his ribs.

"That might take a while." More time than they have, if Miłosz stubbornly sticks to the plan that has slowly been drifting away in recent weeks.

Mx. Zhéng takes a seat at the table nearest Miłosz's desk. None of the regular students have arrived yet, and he's glad for the privacy. "I hope so."

Was that old plan ever something Miłosz *wanted*, or was it just what he thought he needed? Because this feels like want. The warmth blooming like wildflowers through his chest, the desire to have what Mx. Zhéng offers, is more compelling than any reason he ever fabricated for leaving.

The decision isn't made. There's still so much time and so much pain due before he can nail down an answer to where he'll be a year from now.

But he's failed. Despite his best efforts, not only has he found someone to stay for, but he *wants* to. The Miłosz of a few weeks ago would run again.

This Miłosz has a flame licking between his ribs and an empty stomach.

"Let's eat."

# Chapter Nine

The closer they get to Halloween, the more settled Miłosz feels. He had expected the opposite, last-minute scrambling to sort out details and the whatever-this-is with Mx. Zhéng slowly building. It should be stressful.

Instead, he's almost excited. Not quite, but something just to the left of it. Anticipation?

"Everything's almost ready." Miłosz sits on the edge of his dziadzio's bed today, kicking out his feet like a restless child. To dziadzio, that's what he'll always be.

The man is fading slowly. No amount of food fills the hollows of his cheeks, and his face has lost its ever-present flush. A pale, gangly ghost lies here, but the eyes are unchanged. Bright. Proud.

A few weeks ago, those eyes were sad, as if he was watching Miłosz wither away alongside him.

Guilt is a heavy stone to bear. He fought so hard for something that was hurting the one person he's never wanted to hurt. Now that his grip on it has loosened, it's obvious how much Miłosz was hurting them both.

There's still guilt for feeling joy while dziadzio is fading, but it's hard to latch onto when the man finds such deep happiness in seeing it.

"It doesn't look exactly like the concept, but we did our best. We'll take photos from every angle so you don't miss anything."

Dziadzio's gaze drifts down to Miłosz's shirt and back up in question.

"There will be pictures of my costume, too, but I plan to visit you after anyway." Plans were made a week ago to swap visit days with his dziadzio's friends for the holiday.

An idea has been floating around Miłosz's mind for a few days. He hasn't voiced it yet for fear that it might be a *bad* idea. Or, even worse, a *very good* idea.

With Halloween only two days away, now seems like the time to bring it up, whether he's ready or not.

"There is no guarantee they'll agree, but I could ask Mx. Zhéng to join us. You could meet them and see their mystery costume in person." The other teacher deflects every question about their costume. Infuriating.

Dziadzio's face lights up so bright that Miłosz knows he'll be dragging Mx. Zhéng to the care home kicking and screaming if he has to. Except he knows that won't be necessary, because Mx. Zhéng said it themself: they want to know all the things Miłosz likes. And he *loves* his dziadzio.

"I'll ask them tomorrow. We're setting up my classroom after school, then going home to make more krówki."

What Mx. Zhéng doesn't know is that Miłosz has gotten a head start on making his treats. Cooking and cooling the fudge takes a while, and he'll need plenty of it. The school bought candy in bulk for a reason. Teaching Mx. Zhéng will also slow them down.

"I'll make sure they don't destroy your kitchen."

"Your kitchen," a scrawled note insists. The letters become shakier each day.

"My kitchen," Miłosz agrees, not entirely believing it.

Classroom 215 no longer exists.

In its place is a wonderland. *The* Wonderland. Floral arrangements clutter every surface—floor and walls included—while garlands and vines drape from the ceiling. Well-placed lights give the makeshift forest an ethereal glow. The teacher's desk has been cleared to make room for the remnants of an abandoned tea party. There is a sign labeled EAT ME in front of an empty space.

"I'll bring in a wicker basket with the candy tomorrow."

Miłosz looks up from where he's rearranging the tea ware on the desk to find Mx. Zhéng staring again. In the strange light, they look otherworldly. "You're staring again."

"I am." They tilt their head. Miłosz is fairly certain they picked the gesture up from him. "Does it bother you?"

No, not anymore. Getting accustomed to being seen may not have been easy, but it *has* been quick.

He waves a hand dismissively and gets back to work. "Feel free. It's not like you've anything better to do while waiting for me to finish."

At this point, he's stalling. There's nothing of substance left to do here, but he's not ready to go.

It must show in the way his hands flutter around flowers like a bee, because Mx. Zhéng offers an out. "I don't need to come over if you've changed your mind."

"No." Miłosz doesn't take the out. How could he when he's already come this far? Now would be a horrible time for his characteristic stubbornness to fail him. "We can go. I'll grab my bag."

They lock the door behind themselves. Stepping out into the hall feels like regaining normalcy, but not necessarily in a good way. Inside was a magic built by their hands.

Miłosz likes working with his hands. That's why he feels at home in an art room or kitchen; such spaces aren't built for idle hands.

"The krówki recipe we'll use is from my dziadzio's mother," he says conversationally as they walk to his car. Hands brush and twitch but never grasp. "She passed before I was born, but she left behind a recipe book."

Tonight, they'll be reading the recipe from a notecard he translated and transcribed it onto. The original book only comes out on special occasions to preserve it, a small piece of their old home.

The thought follows him through the drive all the way to the kitchen.

"Do you ever hold tight to something because it represents something else you've lost?"

Miłosz busies himself gathering ingredients to give them room to think. It's a big question to ask. Hopefully, the answer implied is enough to justify it.

"No." The answer is slow. Miłosz clutches an old plastic measuring cup tight enough for it to creak. "No. I've never lost anything I love that much."

Oh. Foolishness floods Miłosz's system; he allowed himself vulnerability and finds that he's still alone.

Mx. Zhéng doesn't stop there, though. They lean against the counter, and their shoulders sag from the weight they carry. "I usually hold tight to things that represent what I could never have in the first place."

Neither of them pry. Miłosz has seen the emptiness that Mx. Zhéng fills with plastic smiles; he already knows enough.

This kitchen is the perfect size for two, Miłosz has always thought. His parents and siblings never cared for cooking or baking, so it was always just him and dziadzio. They maneuvered around each other with a practiced ease. Enough space not to trip over each other, close enough for a playful hip bump or a guiding hand on the shoulder.

With Mx. Zhéng, the kitchen has become too big and too small all at once.

It's vexing.

They keep leaning into Miłosz's space to learn where things are or what they do. Whenever he offers a guiding hand, they press heavily into it. He has to apply pressure to avoid being toppled by their cat-like behavior.

It's too much.

It's not enough.

Movies always make such a big deal of the main characters being in close proximity, swelling violins or orchestral crescendos. On screen, their contact seems electric. Miłosz never understood that until now.

Mx. Zhéng presses a hand to the small of Miłosz's back as they read the recipe. His entire self is taken over by the static centering on that one point of contact.

He could ask for space. Mx. Zhéng would even give it, smiling apologetically as they step away. The air between them would grow dense, and neither would mention it.

Wanting that seems foreign to him now. The longer that hand supports his back, the more certain Miłosz becomes that he never truly wanted solitude in the first place. He wanted *peace*, and he was never going to find it alone.

Miłosz turns against the counter to face Mx. Zhéng, their hand sliding to his stomach. He looks up into warm brown eyes and wonders what they want. This isn't the first time he's wondered, but it's the first time the thought hasn't been bitter or wary.

"Tāo," he says, because he's finally made a choice. "What do you want?"

They blink at first, uncomprehending. Miłosz admits to himself that he could have been clearer.

"With me. What do you want *with me*?"

Their gaze softens. The hand falls to their side, and Miłosz doesn't grab it. "I want whatever you'll give me."

He definitely wasn't clear enough. "Not *from* me, *with* me. Together."

How is it possible for their expression to get even softer? They lift a hand and, when Miłosz doesn't flinch or draw back, press it to his cheek.

It feels like sun rays spilling through the leaves of an apple tree. Summer, warm and peaceful, spreading a languid happiness through his limbs.

It feels like connection.

"I want whatever you'll give me," they repeat, voice lower this time. The words are whispered from a mouth close enough to feel the breath of. "What do *you* want?"

Miłosz thinks for a long second, but the answer is clear: "I want to get this drawer knob out of my back."

With the hand on his face, closer to Tāo is the only way to go. The space between their bodies cuts down to an inch. Their faces are even closer.

"Let's get back to work," he whispers, practically into their mouth.

Then the body against him, the hand on his cheek, the breath on his lips, is gone.

Tāo has taken a full step back to create distance between them. Their cheeks burn bright, and their gaze on his face falls lower than his eyes. Somehow, they seem disheveled despite not a single hair being out of place.

The space, and lack of metal digging into the knobs of his spine, lets Miłosz think. He's not sure what he wants in detail, but he knows he wants Tāo. Close, happy, maybe even his.

Having them close was every bit the thrill that movies made it out to be.

It was a lot, tough, and Miłosz is overwhelmed. He takes a deep breath, convinces his cheeks to cool, and raids the cupboard.

They don't talk about anything unrelated to baking until the krówki are set aside to cool.

The time was supposed to clear their heads, and it did, but Miłosz still feels a bit fuzzy. Less moth-eaten, more like butterfly kisses against his heart.

"It needs to cool before we can cut and wrap it." That will take a while, and there is little to do until then. "Would you like dinner while we wait? There's a fairly good pizza restaurant down the street that delivers."

Miłosz hadn't originally intended for them to eat together, but it makes sense. Between staying late to decorate and making the krówki, the sun has set, and neither has eaten.

"Yeah, pizza would be great."

They stand close together at the kitchen counter while scrolling through the online menu. Tāo leans further until they're pressed into Miłosz's side, and Miłosz pretends not to notice even though it sets his heart racing.

A few clicks later, there are no more distractions from the electricity between them.

"We can sit in the living room," Miłosz offers, already halfway out of the kitchen.

The living room is furnished with one couch and three recliners. Deciding where to sit is strategic in a way that he usually doesn't have to think about. If he sits on the couch, it will feel like rejection if Tāo sits anywhere but directly beside him. If he chooses a recliner, it will save him from having to know, but it will feel wrong.

The old, threadbare monstrosities aren't officially assigned to anyone, but only one person ever sits in any of them. With dziadzio moved into the care home, his weekly guests won't frequent the living room anymore, and these seats may never see their unofficial owners again.

Miłosz takes the couch.

He curls into the corner nearest his dziadzio's recliner. The same spot he always ends up in, a creature of habit.

Tāo mirrors him on the far side of the couch. They look sweet like this, run down from a long day but still smiling, feet tucked up under them. Small but content.

Even now, after plenty of time to think, Miłosz doesn't have the words for what he wants. But he does have the words to describe it.

"I want to order food and know I've chosen your favorite, or make us lunch and know you'll enjoy what I made." He stares at his socks as he talks. Black, like every other pair he owns. "I want to know you're thinking about me as much as I'm thinking about you."

Their breath catches, and Miłosz can't help looping up with a playful grin. "I want to believe Babelyn when they say my new hair ties will make you melt."

The soft awe and hope on their face shift to indignation faster than Miłosz can blink. "They gave you those scrunchies to torment me, didn't they? I can't believe my favorite student would do this to me."

Miłosz thinks about the accessories in his desk drawer, the headbands they don't know about. "Yes. I thought they were exaggerating. As..." He pauses to think of a different word, but there's only one. "Affectionate as you've been, there was no reason for me to believe you meant it in the way they implied."

Tāo stares. Keeps staring. Miłosz realizes that either he's an idiot or he's been too deeply steeped in denial to see something in neon flashing lights. Considering how hard he pushed Mx. Zhéng away as they grew closer, it's probably the second.

"I toned it down because you were uncomfortable and going through a lot, but I was absolutely flirting with you. Especially once you started flirting back."

When was that? Definitely when he invited the other teacher to lunch, but what about before that? Initiating handholding at the shops. Asking for help with Halloween decorations. Even as early as when he burst into the auditorium, red-faced at Babelyn's heels, with the excuse of art supplies cradled in his arms.

The when doesn't matter, he decides, because it got him here.

"What now?" Feelings crawl up Miłosz's throat and push the words out. He's ready; he's made a decision, and he's stopped running away from all the things he's afraid of. What now?

They could date. They could fall in love and run off into the sunset together, but dziadzio will still be dying. Will still die. Miłosz will inevitably pull away and lash out because it's the only way he knows how to protect himself. Things will never be perfect.

But they could still *be*.

"What now?" he asks again.

But the doorbell rings, and pizza deliveries are more urgent than not-quite-love confessions.

# *Chapter Ten*

The fresh scent of pepperoni pizza and garlic bread cuts through the lingering sweetness from the kitchen. The television covers the sound of chewing. A movie neither of them is watching plays out, the classic horror movie marathon typical to this time of year.

Never one to speak with his mouth full, Miłosz bides his time.

"That was good," Tāo says when they clear their plate. It goes on the coffee table.

Miłosz takes the cue for what it is.

He faces Tāo fully, no longer pretending to watch a movie he doesn't know the name of. Tāo does the same. They smile.

Miłosz feels a bit like he's drowning, and he's not entirely sure why.

"You asked what I wanted." Tāo leans back with their eyes closed. Head tilted to bare their throat, Miłosz watches the Adam's apple bob as they talk. "From you, and with you. If you're okay with it, I want everything."

Everything. A vast, nebulous expanse.

"Something a bit more specific would be a good place to start."

They worry at the sleeve of their cardigan. Miłosz has quickly learned that all of them are unraveling. This one is more fray than form.

"I'd like for this to be a date."

Miłosz would like that too, but, "If this is a date, will you come sit closer?"

Tāo lifts their head. Brown eyes beg for something being freely given. "May I?"

He nods.

That's all it takes to get Tāo across the couch. They plant themself against Miłosz's side, a wall between him and the rest of the world.

*This is nice*, Miłosz thinks. *I want to keep this.*

The thought is dangerous. It's everything Miłosz strode to avoid when he first moved back here.

With Tāo humming contentedly into his hair, both of them sated and happy, Miłosz can't remember why he was so afraid.

With this to look forward to, the horrors of his future seem more manageable. Still heart-wrenching, but he can see a way to survive it.

Dziadzio was right after all.

Miłosz will never live it down.

Halloween is a tradition they picked up after the move—a piece of American culture dziadzio claimed didn't try to take something away from him.

"Even if dressed as something else, your self is underneath," he'd said on their first Halloween, and little baby Miłosz hadn't understood.

Adult Miłosz, in a hat with rabbit ears, likes to think that he understands now. Far better than his younger self, at least.

"Happy Halloween," he greets the trick-or-treaters passing through during the homeroom period.

"Yes, it's Alice in Wonderland," he tells them when they guess the theme. "We all need to step away from reality now and again."

"I had help," he admits when asked how long decorating must have taken.

The wicker basket on his desk empties, treats wrapped in colorful wax paper going into pockets and backpacks. Miłosz waits until homeroom is ending to add the treats wrapped in blue to the basket.

"You look kind of ridiculous, Mr. J."

Babelyn looks ridiculous themself in a costume that could only have been borrowed from the theater department. They're wearing a green sweater and brown pants to blend in with the tree suit pulled over their clothes. Twigs are pinned to their satchel bag and holding on valiantly.

Miłosz loves being a teacher for the ridiculous moments like this. A rabbit and a tree talking in a field of flowers.

He shrugs. "The secret's out."

There's a moment where they stare with a scrunched-up face, obviously confused, before understanding dawns. They gasp, gape, and finally guffaw.

"I can't believe you! This is perfect!"

He reaches into the basket labeled EAT ME. Two blue-wrapped treats rest in his palm when he holds it out. "Try these ones, Tāo helped make them."

A devilish grin takes over their face. A cartoonish tree shouldn't be allowed to look so evil. "They're Tāo now? No more Mx. Zhéng?" They try to imitate Miłosz, voice pitched low and face pinched into something grumpy.

It would be rude if it wasn't both funny and accurate.

"Given your costume, I assume you saw them before coming here. Surely you've already asked them."

Babelyn crosses their arms over the bulky costume. "Well, yeah, *duh*, but I still want to ask *you*. They're sappy, but you'll give it to me straight." They pause, catching the slip-up. "Straight-forward, obviously not straight. You know what I mean."

He does. Miłosz has never been a romantic, always the pessimist. Sugar-coating doesn't come naturally to him.

"We had a lovely date last night and will be having another this weekend."

"This weekend? What about today? I thought you were having lunch together and seeing your grandfather later or something."

Tāo really did tell them everything. "We are having a normal lunch because I insisted we maintain professionalism at work. And I would prefer that our dates not include family members."

They grimace. "That's fair. I wouldn't want my foster mom around for a date either."

Students start trickling in, and Babelyn takes that as their cue to sit down. "I'll be back tomorrow morning for deets. You can't escape me!"

Miłosz tries to frown, but honestly, he doesn't have many people to talk to about this fragile blooming thing.

The listening ear offered by a tiny sunflower is appreciated.

Even if they make fun of the rabbit ears the entire class.

Tāo said they would be a bit late to lunch, so Miłosz is working on lesson plans when a shadow falls over his desk.

"Nice ears."

Miłosz groans. One more comment and he's removing the hat. "Yes, I made them myself. Now please never mention them again."

There's the scrape of a stool being dragged over. "Why? I think they look quite dashing."

He fully intends to level Tāo with a scowl, but his face twitches and loses the effect when he realizes what he's looking at.

## CANDY APPLES

A clearing of the throat scrapes up a more dignified reaction than staring. "I thought it was the Evil Queen who hands out poisoned apples?"

Tāo smiles through the accusation as they inspect the candy apple in their hands. "It doesn't seem poisoned to me."

For the most part, their costume is classic Snow White: red headband, white-collared blue top, even the yellow shoes. But the skirt has been traded for billowing pants of the same color. To stave off the autumn chill, they even have a cape.

And Tāo, the menace, has the gall to look smug.

"You are ridiculous." Not 'you look ridiculous' because that would be untrue. "But thank you."

He smiles. Tāo smiles back, as always.

What a wonderful thing to have in Wonderland.

"Are you sure I shouldn't change?"

Miłosz adjusts their cape latch when their fidgeting undoes it. "Yes. The whole point is for him to see our costumes. Changing would defeat the purpose of this visit."

Tāo grabs his hands, pulls them to his lips. Moths and butterflies and other beautiful winged things flutter through his chest. "I thought that was an excuse for him to meet me?"

Yes, but Miłosz hadn't realized he was so transparent about it. "No, I couldn't tell him about your costume because you kept so tight-lipped about it. You brought this upon yourself."

They bump gently against his shoulder. "In that case, I'll make sure to apologize."

The care home is decorated for the holiday. Plastic pumpkins and bats litter the place, on desks and hung in windows. Anything that *can* be orange and black is.

They stop in front of dziadzio's door. There's a big sticker of a happy jack-o-lantern under his name.

"Are you sure about this?" Tāo asks one last time.

Miłosz has struggled since his dziadzio's diagnosis, and he will keep struggling. The next few months will be painful. Eventually, all that will be left behind this door is a room full of things to be cleared out.

Right now, his only family is behind that door and excited to see him on their favorite holiday. Excited to meet the person who broke Miłosz out of his self-imposed isolation.

Miłosz is going to cherish this while he can.

He takes Tāo's hand and opens the door.

"Hey, dziadziu, I have someone for you to meet. And you are *not* allowed to say 'I told you so.'"

# *Epilogue*

"He's late."

Tāo paces the left wing of the stage, bursting with nervous energy. The show their class is putting on is small, not even technically an official production, but the students have worked hard on it. *Tāo* has worked hard on it. And their boyfriend isn't here.

"It's not even curtains yet," Babelyn reassures them. As a member of the ensemble, their part is small, and they can afford to be distracted by the fretting teacher. Not that Tāo would admit to fretting. "He'll be here. Drink some water and go check the costumes again."

If they drink any more water, they'll miss the show from constant bathroom breaks. Checking the costumes again isn't an option either because the cast and crew are two seconds away from duct-taping them out of the way.

They've already done all they can to keep their eyes off the reserved front row seat.

"Stop staring at the empty seat, Z. I have a delivery."

Distracted, Tāo turns slowly and doesn't realize how close the delivery is until it grabs their waist to stop a collision. They stare dumbly at their boyfriend, who, by all accounts, *really* shouldn't be backstage.

Miłosz is handsome as always with those piercing green eyes. An apple-print headband, courtesy of their favorite student, holds back messy brown curls and matches the necklace resting against their collarbone.

Beside him, Babelyn is holding a single sunflower like it's something precious.

"I have flowers for you, too, if you can stay upright long enough to receive them."

In Miłosz's other hand, the one not burning through Tāo's dress shirt, is a bouquet of hydrangea blooms in the softest baby blue. The wrapping is black with white polka dots and a satiny blue ribbon.

Tāo is so unabashedly in love with this man.

They press a quick kiss to Miłosz's cheek, careful not to linger with students as an audience, and accept the gift. "Thank you."

Miłosz's cheeks take on a rosy pink that makes Tāo's heart soar. *They* did that. Their boyfriend is so sweet under the stoic facade.

"You're welcome." He leans in for a split-second cheek kiss of his own before stepping back. "Good luck. I hope it's as good as the posters make it seem."

He disappears into the chaos of backstage, and Tāo takes a moment to recenter themself.

Those ridiculous posters.

## CANDY APPLES

At the start of the school year, the two teachers met, and Tāo was instantly drawn in. Something about the new art teacher begged for Tāo to reach out. And they, as a drama teacher, came up with the brilliant idea of an extra credit assignment as an excuse to approach the art teacher for supplies.

Ridiculous, they'll admit.

But it worked! Sort of. Not really, but it got their foot in the door.

And now they're here. Miłosz is sitting front and center in the audience of a show he insisted on painting a backdrop for. The lush green landscape is worlds away from the heartbroken piece that Tāo ruined months ago, even if not intentionally or by their own hand.

"I don't think anything could have saved it," Miłosz said back then.

The resurrected scene on stage argues otherwise.

Tāo brings the gifted bouquet to their face and breathes in. The difficult moments are more than worth it if they pave the way for beautiful ones like this.

# Acknowledgements

This story is a bit of a heartache, so thank you to everyone who carved a little piece of yourself out to make room for it. This includes you, dear reader, but also all of these lovely people.

Thank you Charlie, for using your amazing editing skills to help make this story the best version of itself.

And thank you to my awesome street team crew for your hard work! This book wouldn't be in this many hands without your lovely support. Massive thanks to Fennick Hargrove, Libby May, Alex Larkspur, Alex Moor, and Choci. You're all amazing!

If you've made it this far, thank you again. Hopefully, we can share another journey soon!

www.ingramcontent.com/pod-product-compliance
Lightning Source LLC
LaVergne TN
LVHW041615070526
838199LV00052B/3161